Copycat

I looked at Amanda. 'You know, you don't have to do *everything* Laine does.'

'I don't know what you're talking about,' Amanda said.

'What's that mark on your leg?' I asked her. Just under the hem of her bathrobe I could see a small red line on her shin.

'Nothing,' Amanda said.

'It's a cut,' I said, looking closer. Amanda tried to hide her leg under the table. 'You shaved your legs!' I said.

'Hairy legs are gross,' Amanda said.

I just yelled with laughter.

'Do you want a plaster?' I asked.

'No, I don't,' Amanda growled. 'And don't you dare tell Laine I used her razor.'

'It's not going to work,' I told her. 'You can skip breakfast and shave your legs all you like, Amanda, but you still won't be eighteen.'

'I don't have the faintest idea what you're talking about,' Amanda said airily.

'Sure you don't,' I said. 'Copycat.'

Little Sister books published by Red Fox

LITTLE SISTER

4

Copycat

Allan Frewin Jones

Series created by
Ben M. Baglio

RED FOX

A Red Fox Book

Published by Random House Children's Books
20 Vauxhall Bridge Road, London SW1V 2SA

A division of Random House UK Ltd
London Melbourne Sydney Auckland
Johannesburg and agencies throughout the world

1 3 5 7 9 10 8 6 4 2

First published in Great Britain by Red Fox 1995

Phototypeset in Plantin by Intype, London
Printed and bound in Great Britain by
Cox & Wyman Ltd, Reading, Berkshire
RANDOM HOUSE UK Limited Reg. No. 954009

ISBN 0 09 938411 6

Chapter One

'Hi, folks. I'm Stupendous Stacy Superstar, and I'd like to welcome you to another episode of this network's most popular family show, *I-I-I Don't Belie-e-e-eve It*! Yeeeeeah!' I flashed a big game-show-host grin and Cindy went, 'Brrrrm – *chissssh*!' (Drum-roll and cymbal clash.)

The audience went wild.

'Woo! Yeah! Yo! Yeee-haah!' The audience consisted of my three best friends: Cindy Spiegel, Pippa Kane and Fern Kipsak. The show was taking place in my bedroom. I'm Stacy Allen, *aka* Stupendous Stacy Superstar, game-show host extraordinaire.

I held my hands up to try and quiet down the rowdier elements in the audience. (Fern makes a really good rowdy element.)

'And our first contestant on *I Don't Believe It* this afternoon is the lovely Fern, of Four Corners, Indiana,' I announced. (Four Corners is the town where we all live – but if you're going to do a game-show, you've got to say where the contestants come from, even if they all live within a few blocks of one another.)

Fern got up off the carpet, holding the envelope she'd brought with her. Cindy and Pippa yelled and clapped as Fern came out front.

'And what *really* embarrassing item from your past have you brought to share with us today, Fern?' I asked.

'It's a photo,' Fern said, opening the envelope.

I grinned at Cindy and Pippa. 'I'm sure we'd all love to see your photo, Fern.'

'Pho-to, pho-to, pho-to!' chanted the audience.

Fern took the photo out and held it up.

There was a shriek of laughter from Pippa, and Cindy went, 'Awww! *Sweet*!'

The photo showed Fern, around three years old, curled up asleep on a rug with her thumb in her mouth. Her hair was blonder than it is now and she was wearing a multicoloured sundress.

'Your taste in clothes hasn't improved!'

Pippa shouted. 'I bet you still suck your thumb when you're asleep.'

'I do *not*,' Fern said. But Pippa was right about one thing – Fern *still* wears way-out clothes.

I guess I should explain. *I Don't Believe It* is a game I made up, where each of us has to show the others something really, really embarrassing from when we were little. It can be a picture or a piece of writing or some clothes we used to wear. Or it could be a story about something embarrassing we did. Anything will work as long as it's incredibly embarrassing. Then we mark our scores on the Blushometer to see who's won.

Pippa invented the Blushometer. It's a chart made out of cardboard with bands of colour along it, going from pale pink (hardly embarrassing at all) to a really deep red (*totally* embarrassing).

We each have a place marker, and at the end of the game we see who came up with the most embarrassing thing. Then *they* are the host for the next game.

Fern was the first contestant in this game. She scored a five (out of a possible ten) for her photo.

7

Next up was Cindy, who recited a poem she'd written about her twin brothers, Bob and Denny, when they were toddlers.

'I love my little brothers
Denny and Bob – they're sweet.
Mom and Dad say now they're here
Our family is complete.

I know that when they both grow up
They will be brave and bold.
But right now I'll look after them
Because they're only two years old.'

We all made gagging noises.

'Well, Cindy,' I said. 'That's pretty bad. And believe me, I know what I'm talking about. If my mom wrote stuff like that, we'd *starve*!' One of the ways my mom earns money is by writing greetings-card rhymes.

'I didn't know what my brothers were going to turn out like,' Cindy explained. 'They were fine when they were babies.' Denny and Bob are seven now, and no one in their right mind could describe either of them as *sweet*. Cindy's poem scored a seven on the Blushometer.

Cindy sat down and it was Pippa's turn. She had us all cringing with embarrassment as she told us about the day she was the flower-girl at a cousin's wedding. First of all she spilled a strawberry drink down her dress, and then she stepped on the bride's train and ripped it clean off the back of her wedding dress. Now *that's* embarrassing! Only Pippa could do something like that.

'OK,' I said, 'let's see how the scores look.' I pointed to the Blushometer, which we'd stood up against my desk. 'Fern has a score of five, so she's in last place. Cindy's score is a healthy seven for her yukky poem about her baby brothers. But this afternoon's winner, with a magnificent score of *nine*, is Pippa Kane, for her flower-girl story. Way to go, Pippa!'

'OK,' Pippa said, getting up. 'I guess I'm host now. And I'd like to invite Stacy Allen to share *her* most embarrassing moment with us. Come on down, Stacy!'

I opened my desk drawer and took out a video.

'Whoo!' Pippa said. 'Home movies! It looks like we're in for a treat this afternoon, folks. And how old were you when this video was shot, Stacy?'

'I was about two,' I said. According to the

date scribbled on the label it was filmed eight years ago on vacation in California.

All four of us are ten now. We're in the same grade in school and we're all best friends. It's a good mix – Pippa is really brainy, Fern is kind of a screwball and Cindy is the nicest, kindest person in the world. I'm not sure how I'd describe myself. My thirteen-year-old sister Amanda would probably say I was a skinny, freckle-faced geek with a mouth full of brace. But then I'd describe *her* as an air-headed blonde bimbo – and anyway, who wants to hear Amanda's opinions?

We all marched down to the living room. Before we even got in there we could hear Amanda and her friend Natalie Smith having an argument.

'Eddie Eden makes Cal Hooper look like a total *dog*!' Amanda was yelling.

Eddie Eden was Amanda's current favourite rock star. She was always cutting pictures of him out of magazines and putting them up on her wall, or taping them to her dressing-table mirror. Then she'd sit and drool over them while Eddie Eden's latest tape blasted through the house.

Cal Hooper was the lead singer in a group called Walking on Air. Walking on *Hair* they ought to be called. If Cal Hooper's hair was any longer he'd be able to knit a scarf out of it.

'Get out of here!' Natalie yelled back. 'Cal Hooper is *gorgeous*!'

'He is not!' Amanda howled.

'He is, too!' Natalie yelled back.

My sister and her friends are always having really intelligent discussions like this.

Amanda and Natalie were sprawled all over the couch watching TV. Loud music played while Eddie Eden wandered around in sunglasses on a beach and mimed to his latest song. I pretend to Amanda that I don't like Eddie Eden. That drives her crazy. (I aim to drive Amanda crazy at least once a week – it makes up for all the grief she gives me.)

'Hey, it's the college debating team,' I said, as I walked into the living room with my friends close behind.

Amanda leaned over the back of the couch. 'Stacy,' she said, '*you* think Eddie Eden is better looking than Cal Hooper, don't you?'

'Sure,' I said.

'There!' Amanda crowed. 'Even Stacy agrees with me.'

'Like Frankenstein is better looking than the Wolfman,' I continued. 'I wouldn't want to meet either of them on a dark night.'

11

'It's a waste of time asking *her*,' Natalie said. 'She doesn't know a thing about boys.'

'Are you two planning on staying down here?' I asked. 'We want to watch this video.'

'What video?' Amanda asked.

'This one.' I held it out and she took it.

'Hey, where'd you find this?' Amanda asked as soon as she'd read the label.

'In the closet in Mom and Dad's room,' I told her. I'd seen Benjamin, my cat, slide into Mom and Dad's bedroom and I'd fished him out of the closet just as he was settling down for a nap. Mom doesn't really like him sleeping in their room because he's moulting right now and the hairs get everywhere.

That's when I'd discovered the video tucked away in a box in the bottom of the closet.

'Do you know *why* this was hidden?' Amanda asked. 'It's because it's got Aunt Susie and Uncle Ralph on it. Do you remember that vacation we all went on?'

'Not really,' I said. I could just about remember having watched the video – but that must have been a few years ago, before Aunt Susie and Uncle Ralph got divorced.

'Mom put everything with Uncle Ralph on it away when Aunt Susie came to stay after the separation,' Amanda said. 'Family pictures and everything. So Aunt Susie wouldn't see them and get upset all over again.'

Aunt Susie was unhappy for a long time after Uncle Ralph went to live in Marion. I think she's gotten over it now, but I can remember a lot of tears and whispered conversations with my mom at the time. And I remember my cousin Laine was really upset about it as well. It's easy enough to see why. I mean, I'd just *die* if Mom and Dad ever split up. It's bad enough that Dad has to spend so much time away from home because of his work.

'Put it on,' Amanda said, handing me back the video.

I put the video in the machine. The four of us sat in a row on the rug and I got the machine going with the remote control.

The first scene was a group shot on the beach. There were six of us standing there in swimsuits and waving at the camera. Dad must have been taking the shot.

I didn't remember the vacation at all, and it must have been ages since I'd watched the video. Our one and only Californian vacation and I'd been too young to remember a thing about it!

We'd gone there with Aunt Susie, Uncle

Ralph and Laine. Laine must have been about ten at the time. Like I said, I don't remember anything about the trip, but I've kind of looked up to her all my life.

Like, while I was still wobbling around on my kiddie-bike with the training wheels on, Laine was doing wheelies on a *real* bike. And when we went to visit, she would do fashion parades for us, and give Amanda and me make-overs. She was my absolute *idol*. In some ways she still is, although these days we don't see so much of her.

Behind us, you could see the waves crashing on the golden sand. You could see that the little kid hanging off my mom's arm on the video was me. I was rounder and pudgier in those days – but the flat brown hair was the same, sticking out from under a sun-hat with 'I ♥ California' written on it.

The other guys laughed as five of us waved at the camera, while Laine stood to one side wearing sunglasses and looking really cool.

Mom was talking to the camera – saying something about what a great time we were having. Amanda was pulling at Mom's other arm and yelling to get down on the beach. You know something? Amanda was a real little *princess* even then! She was wearing a pink

14

swimsuit and she had all this curly blonde hair and these big blue eyes. Amanda takes after Mom. I look more like my dad. Brown hair, brown eyes. Oh, well, that's the way it goes.

I fast-forwarded through some shots of scenery and put it back on to normal speed for a scene of Amanda and me playing ball on the beach.

The big beach-ball came bouncing towards me as I stood there wobbling on the sand with my arms out. Whack! The ball hit me in the stomach and I toppled over backward. Amanda and Natalie shrieked with laughter.

There was more stuff of us on the beach. I was holding Laine's hand and she was trying to get me to paddle in the surf. And there was Amanda, jumping around and yelling, trying to get everyone's attention.

There was a wobbly section of film – mostly of legs and feet. Mom's legs, Dad's legs, Laine's legs and Aunt Susie and Uncle Ralph's legs. Amanda must have shot that. You could hear my dad saying, 'Hold it *up* a little, honey.' And Amanda was saying, 'You're not *smiling*! You've got to smile.' As if that made any difference: you couldn't see anything of Mom and Dad above the knees.

Then we came to a shot of Amanda. She

was in some kind of costume. She had on a big old-fashioned bonnet and a frilly white dress. I guess she must have just been in some competition, because she had a blue ribbon pinned to her front.

'Tell us what you did, honey,' came Mom's voice from out of shot.

Amanda beamed out of the TV set. 'I just won first prize in the Little Miss Pioneer Contypishun,' she said, pointing to her ribbon. (She meant 'competition'.) 'I came first of everyone. Which means I'm the best in the world.'

'I don't think we want to see any more of this,' Amanda said from behind me. 'Fast-forward, Stacy.'

'No way,' I said. 'We want to see how you won the contypishun.'

'Fast-forward,' Amanda said. 'Now!'

I ignored her. If Amanda didn't want us to see it, then you can be sure something neat was about to happen.

We all started giggling as Amanda went into her dance routine. You could see how seriously she was taking it from the expression on her face. She hopped up and down and did little pirouettes and jumps.

'Daddy, you're not *watching*!' Amanda came

to a halt, her little fists on her hips and a stern look on her face. 'You've got to watch me!'

'I am watching,' came Dad's voice.

'Everyone's got to watch,' said Amanda, starting her dance all over again.

Cindy and the other guys were yelling with laughter as five-year-old Amanda jumped around in front of the camera. But the loudest laughter was coming from Natalie.

Just then, Amanda on the TV screen got her legs all tangled up and fell in a heap on the ground. Everyone howled with laughter at the expression on her little face. Everyone except Amanda, that is.

'I told you to turn that thing off,' Amanda yelled. (My sister *hates* being laughed at.) She made a dive for me. The next thing I knew, I was flat on my back with Amanda sitting on me as we wrestled for the remote control.

'Help!' I yelled. 'Cindy! Guys! Help!'

I needed reinforcements. And I needed them fast!

Chapter Two

Ladeeez an' gennelmen, you've joined the Indiana All-In Girls Wrestling Championship at a thrilling moment. Amanda 'Mad Girl' Allen has Stacy 'Iron Kid' Allen in a pinfold and is threatening to shove the remote control up her nose. But Iron Kid is fighting back. She's gotten a hold of the remote control. It looks like she's fighting for her life in there. Yes! Iron Kid has gotten out from under Mad Girl.

They're fighting over the remote control as Iron Kid heads behind the couch. This contest could go either way. The crowd is in a frenzy and all bets are off.

Iron Kid is crawling behind the couch now and her trainer, 'Crusher' Spiegel, is shouting instructions from the ringside.

I've never seen a contest like this before. Mad Girl has grabbed Iron Kid by the foot and is dragging her out from behind the couch. Iron Kid is yelling for help! You're not going to believe this.

The audience has invaded the ring! There's complete chaos here, folks! And Mad Girl has gone down with three members of the audience on top of her.

Surely the referee is going to have to stop the contest! It's pandemonium, as Mad Girl's manager, 'Blockhead' Smith, enters the ring and tries to pull a member of the audience off Mad Girl's head. The crowd is sure getting its money's worth today . . .

'Help! I'm being squished!' I yelled from under the whole bunch of them. We hadn't let off steam like this for ages! I was having a great time – until I nearly got Pippa's foot in my mouth. There were arms and legs everywhere, and I could hear Amanda laughing as she tried to pry my fingers off the remote control.

I jerked it away from her and threw it across the floor. It was kind of like one of those fights you see in westerns, where everyone is trying to get their hands on the gun.

'Natalie! Get it!' Amanda yelled.

'Stop her!' I shrieked, wriggling to try and get out from under Amanda.

I'm not too sure what happened then. Natalie made a dive for the remote control and so did Pippa.

'Eeyoww!' Pippa howled as she clashed heads with Natalie.

'Oww!' Natalie yelled.

'Careful!' I shrieked, as the two of them went rolling across the floor and Pippa banged against the little table by the window. I saw Mom's flower vase wobble. I squirmed out from under Amanda and made a dive for it. But I was too late.

Crash! The vase and the flowers and everything else came sailing off the table. It just missed Pippa's head and broke into pieces on the floor, dumping flowers and water and pieces of china all over.

The big fight stopped dead as we all stared at the broken vase.

'It wasn't my fault!' Pippa said. 'Natalie pushed me.'

Right then I didn't really care *whose* fault it was. Mom's favourite vase! White china with these little blue dolphins swimming all around it. It was in pieces.

'Oh, heck!' Amanda panted, scrambling over to the broken vase. 'Mom's going to kill us!'

I sat up, rubbing my ear from where Amanda's knee had whacked me. 'Maybe we can fix it,' I said.

'Oh, sure,' Amanda said sarcastically. 'We'll put it back together with band-aids. Mom will *never* notice.'

Fern crawled over to the mess and started picking the pieces of white china out from the scattered flower stems.

'Maybe we could make a jigsaw puzzle out of it?' she said with a hopeful grin.

'It's not funny,' Amanda said. 'Mom will ground us for the next six months. Stacy, this is all your fault!'

'Mine?' I said. 'I wasn't anywhere near it. It was Natalie!'

'It was *not*,' Natalie said. 'It was Pippa.'

We all crowded around. One half of the vase was OK. The other half was in several pieces.

'We could superglue it,' Pippa said, taking a couple of the pieces of the broken side and fitting them together. 'See?'

Amanda and I looked at each other. I guess the same thoughts were going through both our minds. Only two days ago, Mom had given us a final warning about arguing. Even though we were only horsing around, it had been a *kind* of argument. Mom would go crazy if she found out we'd broken her vase in a fight.

Could we superglue the vase back together so Mom wouldn't notice?

'It's worth a try,' Amanda said. She looked at Natalie. 'Go get some paper towels,' she said. 'We've got to mop all this water up.'

I gathered the flowers together and put them in another vase, while Amanda and the others laid out all the broken pieces on the rug. We were lucky, I guess. The vase had broken cleanly into seven pieces.

'Do we have any superglue?' Amanda asked.

'I've got a tube in my room,' I said. I picked up the fragments. 'Come on guys,' I said. 'Vase-mending party to my room.'

The four of us went upstairs, leaving Amanda and Natalie sponging up as much of the water as they could.

'How's your head?' Cindy asked Pippa.

'Aching,' Pippa said, rubbing the top of her head. 'Natalie's skull must be made of concrete.'

'Yeah,' Fern said. '*Solid* concrete.'

'OK,' Pippa said, kneeling down on my bedroom carpet and lining up the pieces of the vase. 'Where's the superglue?'

I got the tube out of my desk drawer and the four of us sat in a circle on the floor.

'That looks right,' said Pippa as she tested a couple of pieces together. 'Give me the glue.'

'Let Cindy do it,' I said to Pippa. 'We don't want to end up stuck to the carpet.' Pippa might be the brains of our outfit, but she sure isn't practical. Five minutes with a tube of superglue and Pippa would probably have us all glued together like Siamese quadruplets!

Cindy took the tube and put little dabs of glue on the broken edges of the pieces as Pippa sorted them out and handed them to her.

'I heard a story about this guy,' Fern said, 'who used glue just like that to fix one of his shoes. But he put the shoe on before the glue had dried.' She grinned at us. 'He got his foot so totally stuck in the shoe that they had to amputate it.'

'Ew, Fern!' Cindy said, dropping the tube of glue. 'That's gross!'

'Ignore her,' I said. 'She's making it up, aren't you, Fern?'

'Yeah,' Fern admitted. 'But it's the sort of thing that *could* happen.'

Cindy was a lot more careful with the way she held the tube of glue after that.

Gradually, piece by piece the vase came together.

'Uh-oh!' Pippa said. 'That was the last piece.'

'It can't be,' I said. 'There's still a gap.' It was up at the rim. A triangle of china was missing. We hunted around on the floor in case someone was sitting on it. But it wasn't there.

'It must still be downstairs,' I said. 'Heck! We'd better get down there and find it.'

Fern was looking at the half-mended vase with her head tilted to one side. 'Do you really think your Mom isn't going to notice?' she said. 'You can see the seams. She'll spot that it's been glued together in ten seconds flat.'

'Not if we put the broken side toward the window,' I pointed out. 'The other side is fine.'

'But she'll notice the first time she changes the flowers,' Fern said.

'OK, OK,' I said. 'So it's not a perfect plan. But it'll give us time to get down to the mall and buy a replacement. I know the store Mom bought it in. If Amanda and I club together, we'll be able to get a new one, and Mom won't know the difference.'

'My pet goldfish died,' Cindy said, 'and my Mom bought a new one without telling me.' She looked up at me. 'I spotted it right away.'

24

'We're not talking about goldfish,' I said. 'We're talking about vases.'

Cindy shrugged. 'I just thought I'd mention it,' she said.

I heard feet thundering up the stairs, and Amanda came rushing into my room.

'Mom and Dad are back!' she yelled. 'Aren't you finished yet? They'll be in here in *seconds*!'

I stared at her in horror. Oh, boy! If we were going to get out of *this* one, we were going to have to act fast! And I mean *super*fast!

Chapter Three

'There's a piece of the vase missing,' I told Amanda, trying not to panic. 'Did you see it on the floor down there?'

'What? Show me,' Amanda said. Cindy held up the vase and Amanda gave it the once-over. 'We can hide that at the back,' she said.

'We'll have to buy a new one,' I told her.

'What do you mean, *we*?' Amanda said. 'It was your dumb friend who broke it.'

'It was *your* dumb friend who pushed me,' Pippa said.

'We haven't got time to argue,' Amanda said. She ran out with the vase.

I ran out after her. 'We should pay half each,' I called after her as she dashed downstairs. 'Hey, Amanda! Are you listening to me?'

I raced down into the living room. Natalie was on her hands and knees, picking up a few last scraps of leaf and stuff from the wet patch.

There was a heap of screwed-up paper towel on the floor.

'Get rid of that!' Amanda yelled to Natalie. 'Quick!'

Natalie scooped up the soggy towels and ran upstairs. Through the living-room window I could see our car in the driveway. Dad was holding baby Sam in his arms and Mom was taking shopping bags out of the trunk.

I grabbed the flowers out of the other vase and crammed them down in the mended one. Amanda put the vase back on the table, turning it so the cracks didn't show.

'What about the wet patch?' I asked, as I saw Mom and Dad walking up to the front door.

'I don't know,' Amanda said. 'You think of something.'

The front door opened. 'Hey! Girls!' Mom called. 'We're home. We could use a hand with the groceries!'

The two of us stood in front of the table and fixed big smiles on our faces. Amanda gave me a nudge and I quickly hid the spare vase behind my back.

As Mom looked into the living room, I shuffled forward so that I was standing on the dark patch on the carpet.

'Hi, Mom,' we chorused.

Mom stared at us. 'What are you two doing?' she said. 'You look like you're on parade.'

'Nothing,' I said.

'What's happened?' Mom asked suspiciously.

'Nothing,' Amanda said. 'Everything's fine. Everything's just fine.'

For a while, there, we really thought we'd gotten away with it. The vase looked OK from the front and even the wet patch on the carpet wasn't obvious unless you went around the back of the couch. The missing piece was a problem, but as long as Mom didn't take too close a look at the vase before we had time to get down to the mall and find a replacement, we figured we were home free.

I was pretty sure Amanda would go fifty-fifty with me on the cost of a new vase once she'd thought about it. If Mom spotted that the vase had been broken, *someone* would have to own up to it. I wasn't going to take all the blame, and I was sure Amanda wouldn't say it was her fault. Which meant that this was one time when we had to stick together.

But we hadn't figured on baby Sam. Now I want to say at this moment that I really love

28

my baby brother. We *all* love him. He's the cutest thing you could imagine, and he's getting smarter every day. Not so long ago, all he could do was lie in his crib and wriggle. But now he can crawl around the floor. And if you hold his hands, he can even walk a few wobbly steps. Pretty soon, he's going to be walking on his own.

But right then, it was Sam's crawling that caused the problem. Baby brother, I love you to pieces, but did you *have* to take a crawl under that table? Did you *have* to find that missing piece of the vase?

And did you really have to hold it up in your little fist so that Dad would see it?

'What have you got there, sweetheart?' Dad asked. I was carrying a couple of bags of groceries along into the kitchen when I saw Dad go down on his knees behind the couch.

'No, no,' I heard Dad say, 'that's not for little boys to play with. No, that's nasty and sharp. Give it to Daddy, there's a good boy.'

Dad picked Sam up and came into the hall. 'Look what Sam found,' he said to Mom as she came in through the front door.

Mom took one look at the piece of china, then she let out this kind of strangled shriek and ran straight into the living room.

29

Amanda and I looked at each other. We were in trouble.

* * *

'It was an accident,' I said.

'A total accident,' Amanda agreed. 'It could have happened to anyone.'

From the look on Mom and Dad's faces as Amanda and I stood in front of them in the living room, I didn't think they were too impressed by our explanation. Even Dad looked mad, and he hardly ever gets mad at us.

'So how did it happen?' Mom asked.

Neither of us said anything.

'Well?' Mom growled. 'I'm waiting.'

'We tried to fix it,' I said. 'And we'll buy a new one.'

'You can count on that,' Dad said.

'What happened exactly?' Mom asked.

'The table got hit, and the vase just fell off,' Amanda said.

'How?' Mom asked. 'How did the table *get* hit? Who hit it?'

Amanda and I looked at each other.

'You were fighting again, weren't you?' Mom said. Mom really hates it when we fight.

She says we're always fighting. It's not true. Sometimes we don't fight for *days*.

'No,' I said. 'well, not *really* fighting. Not *mad* fighting. We were just kind of horsing around, really, weren't we, Amanda?'

'That's right,' Amanda agreed. 'You see, Natalie was just trying to get Pippa off me, and—'

'Natalie was involved?' Mom said.

'That's right,' Amanda said. 'And she kind of hit Pippa—'

'Natalie hit Pippa?' Dad asked.

'Not on purpose,' Amanda said. 'You see, she was trying to get Pippa and the others off me, and—'

'What others?' Mom said. 'For heaven's sake – how many of you were involved in this?'

'Only Pippa and Cindy and Fern,' I said. 'They're upstairs. You can ask them.'

'There were six of you fighting down here?' Mom gasped. '*Six* of you? Fighting in my living room? What do you think this is – a wrestling ring?'

'We did try to fix the vase,' Amanda said. 'And we're sorry, aren't we, Stacy?'

I nodded.

'What were you fighting about?' Dad asked.

'Well,' I said, 'you know that holiday we had

in California? Well, I was looking for Benjamin this morning, and he'd gone into the closet in your bedroom. You know how he likes to find a quiet place to sleep? And I found him in that box you keep in the bottom in there. That's where the video was. And I thought I could have a game of *I Don't Believe It* with the guys later. It's a kind of game-show thing we thought up, where you have to admit to something embarrassing. You see, I found this—'

'Stop!' Mom said. 'Stop right there.' She looked at Dad. 'This is going to be one of those explanations that give me a headache,' she said.

'It's really simple,' Amanda said. 'Stacy and the others were laughing at my *dancing*. That's why I was trying to get the remote control off her.'

'Natalie was laughing, too,' I reminded her.

'You were dancing?' Dad said in a really baffled voice. 'So where does California come into it?'

'I wasn't dancing *now*,' Amanda said. 'I was dancing *then*. And Stacy was making fun of me in front of her friends.'

'She fell over,' I said. 'It was funny.'

32

'Oh, yeah?' Amanda said to me. 'I don't suppose you ever did anything funny like that when *you* were five?'

'Not in front of a camera,' I said. 'I'm no show-off. Not like you.'

'You're both grounded!' Mom yelled.

We stopped arguing and looked at her.

'You're both grounded for the rest of the week,' Mom said. 'And I don't want to hear another word out of either of you.'

'But you haven't let us *explain*,' I said.

'Out!' Mom hollered. 'And tell your friends to go home right now. *And* you'll be paying for that vase out of your allowances.'

'Gee!' Amanda said. 'A person doesn't even get a chance to *speak* in this house!'

'Out!' Mom yelled. 'Out, before you drive me nuts!'

There are times when my Mom can be so unreasonable. I mean, a person asks you for an explanation, and then won't *let* you explain. Is that fair?

'This is all your fault, you dumb kid,' Amanda hissed at me as we headed upstairs. 'You should have let me do the talking.'

'Oh, yeah? And what makes you think they'd have listened to you?'

'They'd have listened to me, because I'm

not some dorky little kid,' Amanda said. 'They'd have listened to me because I'm *older* than you.'

'Oh, right! I should have stood there and let you tell them how it was all my fault, huh? Sure, Amanda!' I said.

'It *was* all your fault!' Amanda said. 'You and that dumb video.'

'Hey!' Dad shouted from the living room. 'Quit arguing, or you'll be grounded for *two* weeks!'

That sure put a stop to our argument. Next week was Spring Break. We had the whole week off school. No way were either of us going to risk getting ourselves grounded right through Spring Break.

And with Mom on the warpath, it looked like Amanda and I were going to have to be on our best behaviour.

Chapter Four

I went down the hall to Amanda's room on Sunday night – our first grounded night. She was sitting in the 'studio' part of her room. Amanda's room is divided into two areas. One half of it is like a regular (but very messy) bedroom. The other half is filled with her art stuff. One thing Amanda's really good at is art. Come to think of it, apart from cheerleading and gabbing to her friends on the phone, art is the *only* thing Amanda is any good at.

I can spell better than Amanda. I can do math better than Amanda. I can remember things better than Amanda. But I'm no good at drawing and painting and stuff like that. And like it or not, we were *both* grounded.

'What are you doing?' I asked, sticking my head around her door.

'Practising the saxophone,' Amanda said. 'What does it look like I'm doing?' She was at her art desk with a skinny little paintbrush in her hand. She had on her painting smock and she was leaning over a half-finished painting of a terrier dog.

There was a photo of the real dog propped up on the desk.

'Hey,' I said, leaning over her shoulder. 'That's really good. It's just like him.' The photo was of Whisky, our neighbour's yappy little terrier. Amanda had done a really brilliant likeness of him. Right down to that mischievous gleam in his brown eyes. His little pink tongue was lolling out the way it always does. 'What's it for?' I asked.

'Mr Lloyd asked me to do a painting of Whisky for Mrs Lloyd's birthday,' Amanda said. 'He's going to *pay* me! Don't breathe down my neck, Stacy. You're making me nervous.'

'You forgot his whiskers,' I told her. 'And his eyebrows are longer than that.'

'I *know*,' Amanda snapped. 'I haven't finished it yet. What do you *want*, Stacy?'

'I thought maybe we could come to some arrangement about buying Mom a new vase,' I said. 'If we went out and bought a new one, maybe we'd get off being grounded all week. What do you think?'

'I guess so,' Amanda said, dipping her brush

in a little tub of brown paint and mixing it on a saucer.

I perched on the edge of her desk.

'Stacy!' Amanda yelled. 'Don't shake the table.'

'Sorry,' I said.

'You are the world's biggest pest,' Amanda said. 'Now, keep *still*!'

I held my breath and watched as Amanda drew in Whisky's whiskers.

'So are we going to club together for this new vase?' I asked. 'Fifty-fifty?'

'I said yes, didn't I?' Amanda said.

'Good,' I said, jumping off the table. 'We'll go to the mall after school one day this week, OK?'

'You just shook it *again*!' Amanda yelled. 'Will you get out of here!'

'Don't yell,' I said. 'If Mom and Dad hear us arguing we'll be grounded all through Spring Break.'

'I'm not yelling,' Amanda said. 'I'm just asking you nicely to get lost so I can finish this painting.'

'OK,' I said. 'I can take a hint. Do you want me to put a sign on the door? *Do Not Disturb – Genius At Work*.'

'The only person likely to disturb me is you,' Amanda said.

'Hey, Amanda,' I said as I walked out. 'You've got red paint on your nose. You look like a clown.'

'Heck!' Amanda said, rubbing at her nose with her hand. 'Has it gone?'

She'd managed to smear the paint all over her cheek.

'Sure,' I said. 'It's gone.'

I had my fingers crossed that she wouldn't look in a mirror. I kind of liked the idea of my mega-vain sister going around the house with red paint all over her face.

* * *

Amanda and I were on our best behaviour for the next two days. Mom had calmed down about the vase, but that doesn't mean she'd forgotten about it. Amanda found *that* out when she tried to sneak off on Monday night to see her friends and Mom caught her at the door.

'And where do you think you're going?' Mom asked.

'Nowhere,' Amanda said quickly. 'I thought I heard someone ring the bell.' She shrugged. 'I guess I was wrong.'

'I guess you were,' Mom said and Amanda disappeared back upstairs. I guess Amanda had hoped Mom had forgotten about the grounding. Some chance!

You've got to get up pretty early to sneak one past Mom. In fact, you've got to stay up *all night* to sneak one past Mom, and that's the truth.

Dad got home from work late on Tuesday night. He was working in Chicago at the time, and it's a really long drive home, so we'd gotten used to him not being back before we had to go to bed. When Dad has to work in Chicago, there are times when he doesn't even get home *at all* for three or four days in a row. He's a travelling salesman. He sells books direct to bookstores. It means he's away from home a whole lot more than I'd like, although it's not always somewhere as far away as Chicago.

Anyway, I was still awake when he came in to say goodnight.

Benjamin was asleep at the foot of the bed. During the day Benjamin likes to curl up in the laundry basket or in the bottom of a closet, but at night he has to be down at the foot of my bed. So I have to be real careful when I turn over. I mean, I don't want accidentally to tip him off the bed when I change position. When it's really cold in winter I even let him come in under the covers with me. Benjamin's the best bed-warmer you could imagine.

Dad sat on the edge of the bed.

'Hi, honey,' he said, leaning over to give me a kiss. I like it when Dad comes and kisses me goodnight when he's just come in out of the cold. It makes me feel all shivery and happy, knowing he's home. My Dad's got the nicest smile you could imagine. Except that he wasn't smiling. He looked kind of down.

'Bad day?' I asked.

'You could say that,' Dad said. 'I've got to go to New York next week. They want me to attend a big conference over at head office.'

That woke me up real quick. 'But it's Spring Break,' I said. 'I thought you were taking some time off.'

'So did I, honey,' Dad said. 'I was really looking forward to it.'

'Can't you get out of it?' I asked.

'I'm afraid not,' Dad said. 'When the big boss calls, people like me have to jump to attention.'

'How long do you have to be away for?' I asked.

'Monday to Friday,' Dad said. He shook his

head. 'I'm sorry, honey. I know I said I'd be home – but I can't get out of it. They want me there to talk about the work I'm doing in Chicago.'

Major depression! Five whole days. And not just *any* five days – but the whole of Spring Break!

'Can't you call in sick?' I asked.

Dad gave me a bleak smile and shook his head. 'I'll tell you what,' he said. 'The weekend I get back, how about we all take a trip to an amusement park? How would you like that?'

'I guess,' I said. I could see how upset Dad was about having to go to some crummy conference in New York. I tried a brave smile. 'That'll be great,' I said.

It was a real disappointment that Dad wouldn't be home for Spring Break. But that was *nothing* compared to the news that hit us when we got home from school the next day.

Chapter Five

Amanda and I had told Mom we were going to get home a little late from school the next afternoon. But we didn't tell her why. That was going to be a surprise. I had raided my vacation money and Amanda had the money that Mr Lloyd had given her for the painting of Whisky. Between us we had enough (we hoped) to buy Mom a new vase.

We headed for the store that sells china and vases and stuff like that. It's a pretty high-class place, but we hoped they might have something we could afford among all the porcelain figurines and expensive chinaware.

The first problem was that there wasn't a vase like we wanted. White with blue dolphins. The next problem was that the woman assistant had her eyes on us the whole time. We couldn't take a step without her following us around like she expected the vases to just throw themselves off the shelves as we walked past. You could tell just by looking at her with her beady eyes and rock-hard hairdo that she was someone who hated kids.

'I like this one,' I said, pointing to a bright-yellow vase with sunflowers on it.

Amanda shook her head. 'We want to find something similar to the one that got broken,' she said. 'That one's the wrong colour.'

'I like yellow,' I said. (My bedroom walls are yellow. Yellow is my favourite colour.)

Amanda ignored me and wandered off among the glass shelves.

'Now *this* I like,' she said. A creamy-coloured vase with Chinese figures around it.

'Can I help you?' asked the assistant. It was amazing, the way she just *appeared* behind us. Like she'd popped up through a trapdoor in the floor.

Amanda lifted the vase off the shelf, but before she had a chance to look at the price or anything, the assistant grabbed it out of her hands.

'These things are fragile,' she said. 'All breakages have to be paid for.'

'We're not going to break anything,' I said. 'We're just looking.'

'You should price things so people can see,'

Amanda said. 'I was only checking how much it cost.'

'Ninety-seven dollars,' the assistant said, putting the vase back on the shelf. '*Now* do you see why we don't like people meddling with them? How do you think your parents would feel about a bill like *that*?'

Ninety-seven dollars! For a vase! I had the definite feeling we'd come to the wrong place.

'Ninety-seven, huh?' Amanda said, without batting an eyelid. She looked at me, 'I guess that's in our price range, Stacy.'

I caught on right away. I looked at the assistant.

'Can you show us anything a little more up-market?' I said. 'Some of this stuff is kind of tacky-looking.'

'Tacky-looking?' the assistant asked, looking at us like we'd just told her she smelled funny.

Amanda gave a casual toss of her hair. 'We're looking for something stylish for the main hallway,' Amanda said. 'Something that will blend in with our décor.' She smiled. 'Something to set off the Chippendale cabinet at the foot of the main stairway.' She looked at me. 'And it will have to blend in with the paintings, won't it, Stacy? The Van Goghs and the Gauguins.'

The only pictures we had in the hall were a couple of photoprints of New England in autumn – and I'm pretty sure Van Gogh and Gauguin hadn't taken the photos. But it was kind of funny to let the snooty assistant think we came from a home that had stuff like that in it.

'I'm afraid our maid broke the vase we used to have there,' Amanda told her. 'Mother was terribly upset. It was an antique. Over one hundred years old.'

The assistant gave us a strange look. I couldn't tell if she'd swallowed Amanda's story or not. It was all I could do to keep a straight face.

'I'm sure we can find something suitable,' the assistant said.

'I hope so,' Amanda said, giving me a sly nudge. 'It'll save taking the Rolls-Royce down to the city.'

'Oh, we don't want to do *that*,' I said. 'I've got to get back for my showjumping competition.'

We were in that shop for half an hour, pretending we had all the money in the world, Amanda even got the assistant to write down a list of prices of stuff we couldn't have afforded in a million years while we talked about our swimming pool and the twenty or so rooms we had in our mansion.

The only problem was that after all that boasting, we couldn't ruin it all by buying anything we could afford.

'Thank you,' Amanda said after the assistant had shown us just about every expensive thing in the shop. 'We'll have to discuss it with Father.' She gave a big smile. 'I expect we'll send the butler over to pick something up later.'

We left the shop and ran around the corner, bursting with laughter.

'That'll teach her to come over all hoity-toity,' Amanda giggled. 'Did you see her face when we said we lived in Roseway?' Roseway is the part of town where all the really rich people live.

'But we still haven't got a vase,' I pointed out.

'We'll find some place else to buy one,' Amanda said.

I looked at my watch. 'We're really late,' I said. 'And we're supposed to be grounded. Mom will kill us.'

We tried to think up some excuses on the

bus ride home. But the way things worked out, we didn't need any excuses.

We were in for a big shock.

The front door was open and Mom was standing there with this worried look on her face.

'*There* you are!' she said, looking really relieved.

'We told you we'd be late,' I said. 'We've—'

'Your grandmother has had an accident,' Mom said. 'I've left Sam with Mrs Lloyd.'

'An accident?' Amanda asked. 'A *bad* one?'

I got this horrible icy feeling in my stomach.

'She's done something bad to her ankle,' Mom said. 'Hop into the car. We're going to see her.'

'How did she do it?' I asked, as we piled into the back of the car and Mom got the engine running.

'Reaching for something, so your grandpa said,' Mom told us. 'She got up on a stool. I'm always telling her to use steps!' Mom sounded terribly concerned.

Grandma and Grandpa Whittle are my mom's parents. They live over the other side of town. (Our other grandparents, Grandma and Grandpa Allen, live over in Illinois so we don't see quite so much of them.)

Grandma and Grandpa are the nicest people you could imagine. Grandpa is real funny and he knows all these great tricks. Like he'll wave his hands in front of your face and then pull a candy bar out of your *ear*. And you can never see where the candy bar came from. The problem with Grandpa, though, is that he's recovering from a bad heart attack. It's not that he's ill *now*, but the doctors have told him he's got to take extra care of himself. (What this really means, is that *Grandma* has to take extra care of him.)

The thought of poor Grandma having a bad fall made me feel really queasy inside.

We got to their house in double-quick time. Grandma was lying in bed with a big bandage around her ankle. Grandpa was sitting by the bed, holding her hand and looking real upset.

'Mom!' our mom cried as we ran into her bedroom. 'I can't leave you alone for five minutes! What on earth do you think you were doing?'

'She was up on a stool straightening a picture,' Grandpa said. 'I told her to leave it. She doesn't listen to me.'

'My favourite grandchildren,' Grandma said, with a big smile. 'Isn't this nice?' She reached out her arms as Amanda and I ran over to the bed to give her a big hug.

'Careful, you two,' Mom said.

'Ssh!' Grandma said, hugging us. She was a little pale, but otherwise she looked fine. She winked at us and looked at Mom. 'It was just a little fall,' she said. 'Your mom likes making a fuss.'

I'd been sitting in the back of the car having all these nightmare visions of what Gran might look like. I was so relieved to see she wasn't badly hurt that I had to wipe away a couple of tears. Amanda looked kind of choked up as well.

'No wonder I get in a state!' Mom said. 'You shouldn't take risks like that at your age.'

Grandma just smiled. Grandma is always smiling. She's the kind of person who could be in an earthquake, and she'd just say, 'Well, wasn't *that* something!' and start cleaning up without batting an eyelid.

'How bad is it?' Mom asked.

'Let's say I'm not going to be doing any *dancing* for a few weeks,' said Grandma. 'The doctor said it's a bad sprain.' She patted Grandpa's hand. 'We'll be OK.'

'You two are worse than kids,' Mom said,

with a relieved laugh. 'What am I going to do with you?'

'Ben will look after me,' Grandma said, squeezing Grandpa's hand. Grandpa smiled, but I could see from his eyes that he was worried. Since his heart attack, Grandma had been looking after *him*.

We stayed over there for an hour or more. Out in the hallway, Grandpa and Mom had a long, whispered conversation.

'I'll see what I can do,' Mom told him. 'Give me a call tomorrow and I'll come over, OK?'

In the car on the way home, Mom told us what Grandpa had been saying. He was really worried that he wouldn't be able to look after Grandma properly, and they couldn't afford a home nurse.

'I promised to go over and see what I can do tomorrow,' Mom said. She shook her head. 'You know how bad Grandpa is at looking after himself at the moment. Your grandmother does everything.'

Amanda and I made dinner that night, to give Mom a rest. And then we went up to Amanda's room and spent the rest of the night making Grandma this real nice get-well card.

Amanda drew a cartoon of Grandma sitting at home with her leg up, eating candy and watching TV while Grandpa was vacuuming the carpet behind her. Then we made a heart-shape around the cartoon with glue and poured silver and gold glitter over it.

I wrote *With All Our Love To Grandma. Get Well Soon* in my neatest handwriting.

Then we took it down to Mom so she could write a rhyme for inside. My Mom writes rhymes professionally. For greetings cards. That's one of her jobs. The other is proofreading. You know, checking books for spelling mistakes and stuff. She works down in our basement, which Dad converted into a neat little office for her. That way she can work and keep an eye on Sam at the same time.

Mom laughed at Amanda's cartoon (Amanda had done a really good likeness of Grandma and Grandpa), and then wrote inside:

> 'Gran Whittle, Gran Whittle, you must take more care
> And not stand on stools when you reach in the air.
> Now you have to rest and let us take the strain
> In no time at all, you'll be dancing again.'

* * *

Mom took the next afternoon off from working to go over to Gran's house. She was home by the time Amanda and I got in from school.

'Is everything OK?' Amanda asked right away.

Mom was sitting at the kitchen table. She looked worried all over again.

'Not really,' Mom said. 'I'm worried about your Grandpa as much as anything. I really don't think he's up to looking after your Grandma all by himself. I rang your Aunt Susie to see if she could stay over with them for a few days to help out. She says she can help out until Monday.' Aunt Susie works full time – I guess she couldn't get any time off at such short notice. She lives in a town a few miles away.

'The thing is,' Mom continued, 'I've told your Aunt Susie that I'll take over next week. I've kind of promised.' Mom looked at us. 'Which means I'll be staying over at Grandma's for a few days. That way, I can look after her and keep an eye on your Grandpa at the same time.'

Amanda's eyes lit up. 'And Dad will be

away, too,' she said. 'So we'll be here on our own.' I could see what was going through Amanda's mind. No Mom. No Dad. Parties! Late nights! Freedom!

Mom shook her head. 'I can't leave the two of you here alone,' she said.

'So, will we be staying at Grandma's house?' I asked.

'There's isn't the room,' Mom said.

'Don't worry about us,' Amanda said. 'We can look after ourselves. No problem.'

'I can't leave you on your own,' Mom said. 'It's illegal to leave children all on their own.'

'I'm not a child.' Amanda sounded offended. 'And I can make sure Stacy doesn't get into any trouble.'

'Hmmm!' Mom said. 'And I get home to find the house wrecked and the two of you trying to kill each other. I don't *think* so, Amanda.'

'You don't trust us!' Amanda said. 'You don't even trust your own daughters.' She put her arm around Mom's shoulders. 'I'm thirteen, Mom. I'll be able to cope.' She looked at me. 'We'll be able to cope, won't we, Stacy?'

'I guess,' I said uncertainly. I was already having visions of what my life would be like with Amanda in charge. *Stacy Allen: Prisoner Number 1856943.*

'It's not a case of whether I can trust you or not,' Mom said. 'You have to be properly looked after. It's all arranged.'

'What have you arranged?' Amanda asked.

'Your cousin Laine is coming over here for the week to look after you,' said Mom.

'Laine?' Amanda asked. 'But she's in college in Marion.'

Mom shook her head. 'She's got two weeks off for Spring Break. And she's already agreed to come over here and stay with you for the week while I'm looking after your grandmother.'

'Really?' Amanda said with a big smile. 'That's great!'

Great? I wasn't so sure. Remember I said she was still my idol in a way? Well, that's true – but Laine had changed a lot over the past few years. She'd become the sort of teenager that Amanda admires, rather than the kind of person *I'd* want to be when I'm eighteen.

I wasn't sure how much I was going to enjoy a whole week with cousin Laine.

Chapter Six

It's edge-of-your-seat time again as we take you on another journey with the one – the only – Stupendous Stacy Superstar, in the continuing adventures of Stacy In Peril.

We left our heroine as the forces of evil conspired to make Spring Break a total washout!

In a gloomy office somewhere in New York, a faceless executive chuckled with delight as he added our heroine's father's name to the list of employees forced on to the treadmill of the deadly Annual Conference.

And in a small house in Four Corners, Indiana, a nasty little gremlin jogged the stool just as an innocent grandmother reached up to straighten a picture, and our heroine's mother leaped to the rescue. Does the cruelty of these dark forces have no limit?

And as if that wasn't enough, see how our brave heroine's best friends are taken away. Pippa Kane: out of town, staying with her father in Evansville.

Cindy Spiegel and her whole family heading north to Lake Michigan. Fern Kipsak off visiting relatives for the entire week.

Unless some miracle happens, it looks like our heroine is going to be left in the clutches of the Wicked Big Sister.

But look! Even as the dark clouds are gathering, a light is seen on the horizon. The forces of darkness quake and quiver in fear as the light speeds towards Four Corners. Is it a flashlight? Is it a shooting star? No! It's Laine Shelby Baxendale, speeding to the rescue.

At least, I *hoped* that was what she was going to do. I hoped she wasn't going to be just another *problem*!

★ ★ ★

'I think it's going to be OK,' I told Benjamin as he sat on my lap for me to comb him. 'I know Laine has changed a little in the last few years, but I'm sure we'll get on just fine.'

Benjamin purred in agreement.

'I mean, maybe Laine *has* got a little self-centred. And maybe she did kind of ignore me that last time I saw her – but that's only because she was real busy,' I told him. 'I'm sure she's still really nice *underneath*. And what if she did talk about herself all the time? I guess *I'd* talk about myself if I was doing all the interesting things Laine is doing right now. You know, going to college and stuff.'

I pulled the clumps of cat hair out of the comb and rolled him over so I could brush his other side.

'You are losing so much hair!' I said, as the comb filled up with a whole bunch of his grey fur. Benjamin is a Russian Blue. That's a *pedigree*. He might act like an alley cat sometimes, but deep down he *knows* he's special.

'I know you've never met Laine,' I told him. 'But you'll get used to her – and she's bound to like you. Nice people always like cats.' I got Benjamin as a present two Christmases ago. He was *very* expensive, but there was more money around in those days. That was before Dad's firm closed down the local office and he had to start making those long trips up to Chicago. And it was before Mom went back to the work she'd done before she started a family.

'Ow! Benjamin!' I said as he started kneading at me. 'I wish you wouldn't *do* that.' He's got such sharp claws. It's like having a bunch of needles stuck in your legs when he gets going. Purr purr. Knead knead. Claw claw.

'That's it,' I said, lifting him off my lap and dumping him on the bed. I frowned severely at him. 'Bad cat!'

He rubbed up against me. It's no good – I can't be mad at Benjamin for more than a couple of seconds. I cleaned out the comb and petted him.

You know, I've got this real good way of telling whether I'm going to like anyone. I just ask them if they like cats. Nice people *always* like cats.

Have I mentioned that Amanda doesn't like Benjamin much? She doesn't actually *dislike* him, but she's definitely not a real cat person. Not like me. Now, I'm a cat person. So are all my best friends. So Laine *had* to like Benjamin – I just knew it.

* * *

Monday morning was kind of hectic. It was the first real day of Spring Break. I know I'd already had the weekend off from school, but that doesn't count, because I always have weekends off. The real fun of being on the Break starts on Monday morning when I wake up and know that I don't have to get up and head for school.

Something I like to do on my first morning

off school is to wake up as if it was a normal Monday.

'Heigh-ho, another Monday morning. Come on Benjamin, it's time to get up. What classes do I have this morning?'

None! No classes at all! I'm on vacation! Yeaaay! And then I curl up under the bed-covers again and think about all the things I can do for the next week.

I didn't hang around in bed on this particular Monday morning. There was too much going on. Dad was at the kitchen table sorting out a whole heap of papers and documents. Mom was writing out a list of the meals she'd prepared and put in the freezer for us.

'I've labelled everything,' she told me. 'There's enough food in there to keep you going all week, but in case you run short of anything, I'm going to leave some money with Laine.'

'Lots of money?' I asked hopefully, already dreaming up treats and outings.

'No, not lots,' Mom said. 'Enough.'

'Are you sure enough will be enough?' I asked. 'What about unexpected expenses?'

'What kind of unexpected expenses?' Mom asked.

'I don't know,' I said. 'If I knew what they'd be, they wouldn't be unexpected, would they?'

'I'll give you some extra spending money,' Dad said.

Just then, Amanda came running into the kitchen.

'Does Laine have a car?' she asked. 'I've thought of loads of places she could take us.'

A car! I hadn't thought of that. We could take trips out into the country for picnics. We could go to the wildlife park.

'No,' Mom said. 'She doesn't have a car.'

'Aw!' Amanda's face fell.

Dad laughed. 'It's lucky for her she hasn't,' he said. 'Knowing you two, you'd have her driving you around all week.'

'Actually,' Mom said, 'Susie did mention that she's thinking of buying Laine a car sometime soon. Susie said Laine is taking driving lessons.'

'That's no good,' Amanda said. 'We need a car *now*. Mom? Couldn't you leave your car here? Laine could drive us around in that.'

'No, I couldn't,' Mom said. 'Laine hasn't passed her test yet. She's not allowed to drive.'

'What kind of eighteen-year-old doesn't drive?' Amanda asked. 'I've told all the guys we'd be going out cruising.'

I bet she had! I bet she'd been bragging like crazy about rides all over town. I was suddenly quite glad Laine *didn't* have a car. I could see it all. Amanda and the entire Bimbo Brigade crammed into the car, and me stuffed in the trunk because there wasn't enough room.

'You can go for rides,' Mom said. 'On a bus. Or on your bike.'

'Huh!' Amanda said. 'What's the point of being eighteen if you don't have a car?'

Amanda went off in a huff. Laine had already let her down, and she hadn't even arrived yet!

Not long afterwards, we all went outside to wave goodbye to Dad as he put his case in the back of the car and set off for the airport. Then Mom started rushing around getting stuff together for her week with Grandma and Grandpa while Amanda and I played with Sam.

Then the four of us got into the car and headed for the train station to pick Laine up.

* * *

Laine was standing in front of the station. I saw her first and jumped out of the car.

'Laine!' I yelled, jumping up and down and waving. 'Over here!'

Laine is really good-looking. She was always pretty, but now she had the figure to go with it. The way Amanda is beginning to fill out in all the right places makes me feel like a beanpole sometimes. But up against Laine, Amanda was about as curvy as an ironing-board. I mean, Laine is a *real* teenager, not a wannabe like Amanda.

She was dressed all in black. Black jeans and a black T-shirt under a black denim jacket. And she had this long curly blonde hair, which was quite a surprise, because her hair used to be light brown. She must have dyed it blonde recently. I had to admit, it looked real neat.

'Hi, everyone!' Laine called, waving and picking up her duffel bag as she came over to us. Amanda got out of the car and we both gave her a big hug.

'This *is* good of you, Laine,' Mom said. 'Girls, put Laine's bag in the trunk.'

Amanda and I had a quick battle over who got to the duffel bag first while Laine cooed over Sam.

'Isn't he *big*?' Laine said, lifting Sam up and giving him a kiss. She smiled. 'The last time I saw him he was so tiny!'

'They do grow,' Mom said with a laugh. 'Of course, you haven't seen him for months.'

'Mom showed me some pictures,' Laine said. 'I keep meaning to come and visit, but you know how it is, with college and everything.' She looked at us. 'And you've grown, too,' she said. 'Amanda – you must be fifteen now.'

'Thirteen,' Amanda said, with the biggest smile I'd ever seen on her face.

'Well, you sure *look* fifteen,' Laine said. 'At *least*! Doesn't she, Aunt Barbara?'

'Don't say things like that,' said Mom. 'The older these two look, the older I *feel*!'

'I've grown, too,' I said.

Laine nodded. 'I can see that,' she said. 'You're getting real tall, Stacy.'

'Everyone is growing like crazy,' Mom said. 'And I've got the grey hairs to prove it.'

We all piled into the car, Laine in the front and Amanda, Sam and me in the back.

On the drive home, Mom asked Laine about Uncle Ralph. (Laine was living with him in Marion while she studied at college over there.) Laine said he was fine, and that he had a *sort-of* girlfriend, although she wasn't sure if it was serious or not.

'What's college like?' Amanda asked, leaning over the back of Laine's seat.

'It's great,' Laine said. 'I've got lots of friends there. We have a real good time.'

'Is it like school?' Amanda asked.

'Kind of,' Laine said. 'But better. You get a lot more free time. There are lectures, of course, but you're mostly left to plan your work out yourself.'

'Do you get homework?' I asked.

'You have to work on your own a lot,' Laine said. 'You know – writing papers and stuff like that. There's a huge library. You'd love the sports facilities, Amanda, if you're still into all that running around.'

'Hear that?' Mom said to Amanda. 'You have to work on your *own*. Do you think you could manage that?'

'Easily,' Amanda said with a toss of her hair. (Ha! That'll be the day!)

'Do you get to meet lots of boys?' Amanda asked, her eyes getting bigger and bigger.

'Sure,' Laine said with a grin.

'Do you have a boyfriend?' Amanda asked.

She *would* ask that. Sometimes I can't believe my sister. (Sometimes? *All* the time.)

'I guess you'd call him that,' Laine said. 'His name's Matt. I'll show you a picture of him later. He's OK.' She looked at Mom. 'Actually,' she said, 'Matt said he might be able to come over during the week. Would that be OK, Aunt Barbara?'

'Sure,' Mom said.

'Does he have a car?' Amanda asked. I knew why she asked *that* question. She still had dreams of cruising around. Amanda, Laine and Matt – three teenagers out on the town!

'Yes,' Laine said.

'Great,' Amanda said, leaning back and giving me a poke with her elbow. 'A car!'

We got home and Mom gave Laine a quick run-through of the house routines while Amanda and I loaded Sam's stuff into the back of the car.

'Don't let them wear you out,' Mom told Laine as we all stood out in the driveway to wave goodbye. She looked meaningfully at us. 'I'll call every day,' she said. 'Behave, OK?'

'It'll be fine, Aunt Barbara,' Laine said. 'Give my love to Grandma and tell her we'll be over to visit.'

Mom strapped Sam into his car seat.

'Amanda,' Mom said, 'no wild parties, you hear?'

'I wouldn't dream of it,' Amanda said.

'And clean up after yourselves – both of you,' Mom said.

'Mom! it'll be OK,' I said. 'Get out of here!'

Mom gave Laine a last anxious look as she got into the car.

She wound down the window. 'And no fighting!'

Laine put her arms around our shoulders.

'I'll look after them,' she said. 'Don't *worry*, Aunt Barbara. Everything will be just fine!'

'You don't know what you're letting yourself in for,' Mom called, as she drove out into the road. She gave a final wave.

'Well,' said Laine, ushering us into the house. 'What have you got planned?'

'Nothing,' said Amanda. 'We can do whatever you like.'

'Don't you have friends you want to go and see?' asked Laine.

'Sure,' said Amanda. 'They're all *dying* to meet you.'

I didn't think Laine looked too thrilled by this. I could understand it – meeting Amanda's Bimbo Brigade wouldn't have made my day, either.

'Oh, sure,' said Laine. 'I'll meet your friends sometime. But not right now, huh? I'm kind of tired from the trip. I was going to lie down upstairs. You know, read a magazine. Unwind a little.'

'I'll show you your room,' Amanda said.

'You're sleeping in Mom and Dad's room. I'll show you where everything is.'

'I know where everything is,' Laine said. 'I *have* been in this house before.'

Maybe I imagined it, but I thought Laine sounded a little ratty. Almost as if she couldn't be *bothered* with us.

Of course, Amanda didn't notice anything. A person would have to have a sign with *Shut up, Amanda!* written on it in neon before she'd get the message.

'You haven't seen *my* room recently,' Amanda said.

'I'll see your room later,' Laine said. 'I just want to unpack and take a rest.'

'I'll help you unpack,' Amanda said, grabbing Laine's duffel bag and racing upstairs with it. 'Follow me!'

Laine followed her up.

'You're so energetic, Amanda,' Laine said. 'I feel tired just *watching* you!'

I went up after them.

If Laine felt tired after two minutes of Amanda rushing around, what was she going to be like after a whole week?

Chapter Seven

'Mom emptied out some drawers for you,' I told Laine as we went into my parents' room.

'And there's space in the closet,' Amanda said, opening the door. 'We'll help you with your stuff.' I knew that Amanda was dying to see what clothes Laine had brought.

Laine opened her bag. She had some real nice clothes. I took out a gorgeously soft lemon-yellow sweater.

'It's cashmere,' Laine said as Amanda gave it a stroke.

'I'll put it in the drawer,' Amanda said.

'*I'll* do it,' I said, grabbing one of the arms.

'Don't *do* that!' shouted Laine as we fought for possession of the sweater. 'You'll ruin it!'

Boy – that stopped us in our tracks. I hadn't realized Laine could be so snappy. Maybe she really *was* tired after her trip – Mom always gets snappier when she's tired.

'It's very expensive,' Laine said, taking the

sweater from us and giving us a big smile. 'You wouldn't want to have to pay for a new one for me would you?'

'Sorry,' we both said.

Phew! Note for the diary: *Don't mess with Laine's clothes!*

'That's OK,' Laine said, folding the sweater into a drawer. 'There's no harm done.'

'Oh, wow,' Amanda said, lifting a maroon bag out of Laine's duffel bag. 'Is this all your make-up stuff?'

'That's right,' Laine said. 'Careful with it, Amanda – there are some bottles of perfume in there.'

'Can I look?' Amanda asked. 'I could put all the stuff out on the dresser for you.'

'OK,' Laine said. 'You do that. And, Stacy, you can put things in the drawers, as long as you're careful. And I'll hang the other stuff in the closet.'

I filled the drawers with Laine's things. Amanda was sitting at the dressing table, drooling over Laine's make-up. There were lipsticks and face creams and small boxes with different-shaded eye-shadow. Three different deodorant sprays and a whole bunch of eau de toilette bottles and perfume with names like Moonglow and Orchidee.

'Wow,' Amanda breathed, taking out a razor. 'Do you shave your legs, Laine?'

'Yes,' Laine said. 'Hairy legs are real gross.' She carefully unfolded a long deep-blue shirt and carried it over to the closet.

'Will you show me how to do it?' Amanda asked.

'You don't have any hair on your legs,' I said.

'I do too!' Amanda said.

'Where?'

Amanda pulled up the leg of her jeans. 'There!'

As far as I could see, her leg was about as hairy as a pool ball.

'Aaiiee!' Laine screamed, taking a leap backward from the closet. 'Something *moved*!'

A furry grey face peered out from under Mom's clothes.

'It's OK,' I said, running over to the closet and kneeling down to haul Benjamin out of there. 'You know you're not supposed to sleep in there,' I told him. 'Bad cat!' I picked him up and stood up. 'It's only Benjamin,' I told Laine, holding him out for her to stroke.

Laine backed away, waving her hands.

'Don't bring it near me,' she said.

I smiled. 'He's not an *it*, Laine,' I said. 'He's

a *he*.' I rubbed Benjamin's head. 'See what you did?' I told him. 'You scared Laine. You say you're sorry!'

'Stacy – don't bring it near me,' Laine said. 'I'm allergic to cats.'

I stared at her. Benjamin gave a wriggle and jumped down on to the carpet. Laine backed away around the bed, looking at Benjamin as if he was a huge spider or something.

'He won't hurt you,' I said. 'He's the nicest cat in the world.'

'Don't you believe it,' Amanda chipped in. 'He's a terror.'

'Just take it out of here, please, Stacy,' Laine said. 'I really can't stand cats anywhere near me.'

I couldn't believe this. Laine didn't like cats? How could anyone not like cats?

I picked Benjamin up again and dropped him outside the door. He gave me an offended look and sat down in the hallway to groom himself.

'Didn't Mom tell you about Benjamin?' I asked. 'I got him a couple of years ago.'

'No. She didn't,' Laine said, crossly.

'Can I try some of your perfume?' Amanda asked, sniffing at one of the bottles as if nothing had happened.

71

'Not that one!' Laine yelled, snatching the bottle out of Amanda's hand. 'Do you have any idea how much that *cost*!'

'I'm sorry,' Amanda said in surprise. 'I was only going to have a sniff.'

'Yeah, well, not this one,' Laine said, putting the bottle down at the back of the dresser. 'Here you go – you can try this one. I got it for Christmas. It's not really me, but you might like it.'

I waited for some comment from Amanda, but she was too busy sniffing at the bottle.

'It's smells nice,' Amanda said.

'You can have it,' Laine said. 'I never wear it.'

'Really?' Amanda breathed. 'I can really have it?'

Laine nodded.

Big deal, Amanda, I thought. *She's already said she doesn't like it. She's just dumping it on you, and you're too dumb to notice.*

Still, if Amanda wanted to go all starry-eyed about it, that was up to her. I had my own things to think about.

I did my best not to be offended that Laine didn't like cats. Maybe some people can be nice without liking cats. But it was a little hard to understand.

Laine dabbed some of the perfume behind Amanda's ears and on the insides of her wrists.

'Don't smell it yet,' Laine said. 'Let it dry first. Give it a few seconds to react with your skin and then take a sniff.'

Amanda rubbed her wrists together then sniffed.

'Wow, that's lovely,' she said. She held her wrist out to me. 'Smell this, Stacy,' she said.

I took a careful sniff – expecting it to be one of those really sweet smells that Amanda likes to douse herself in when she's going somewhere special. (Sometimes you can smell Amanda coming for three blocks.) But it wasn't bad.

'Let's find one for you, Stacy,' Laine said. She picked up a dark-blue bottle. It reminded me of the kind of bottle you see in pictures of *Arabian Nights* scenes – round at the bottom with a long, skinny neck and a glass stopper.

'This is Scheherazade,' Laine said, as she dabbed a drop on my wrist. 'This one drives the boys wild.'

'Don't wear it in front of Davey Brown,' Amanda said. 'He'll start following you around again.'

'Who's Davey Brown?' Laine asked with a smile.

'A kid who lives across the street,' I said. 'Amanda's just trying to be funny.'

'Which one drives the boys wilder?' Amanda asked with a grin. 'I want to drive boys wild.'

Laine smiled. 'Any boy in particular?' she asked.

'Nah,' Amanda said airily. 'I like to play the field.'

'Huh!' I said. 'You mean you'd like to try,' I looked at Laine. 'Amanda doesn't have any boyfriends.'

'Only for the time being,' Amanda said. 'Plenty of boys are interested in me.'

'Name one,' I said.

Amanda ignored me. I knew she'd been aiming to catch a boy ever since she'd found out that her arch rival at school, Judy MacWilliams, had a boyfriend. But if she'd found one, she certainly hadn't told me. And, believe me, Amanda would have told me *all* about it.

Amanda looked around at Laine. 'Will you show me how to make myself up?' she asked. 'So I look as good as you?'

'I suppose I could try,' Laine said.

'Right now?' Amanda asked.

'Let me have a rest first,' Laine said. 'We'll do it some other time. We've got all week. But

I would like something to eat. I haven't eaten yet today.'

'Did you skip breakfast?' I asked.

'I don't eat breakfast,' Laine said.

'You *don't*?' Amanda said. 'Nothing?'

'Just a cup of black coffee,' Laine said. 'I can't face food before noon.'

'Mom put a pasta salad in the fridge,' I said. 'Do you want some of that?'

'That would be just fine,' Laine said.

I went down to the kitchen. Benjamin was lying on a chair in there with his legs in the air and his head hanging upside down as he watched a fly zipping around. He's funny like that. He'll watch flies and moths and things for ages without ever trying to catch them. I mean, a fly could come and do the Mexican Hat Dance an inch away from Benjamin's nose and he'd just sit there watching it.

I got the bowl of salad out of the refrigerator and set three places.

A few minutes later, I heard Amanda and Laine coming down. Benjamin heard them too, and headed straight for the cat-flap. I think that cat must know when he's not liked.

'Benjamin, there's no need to—' Too late. Back legs and tail disappeared through the cat-flap. Oh well, I guess it was for the best.

Maybe Laine would get used to Benjamin after a while. No one could dislike Benjamin once they got to know him.

'What kind of music do you listen to?' Amanda asked Laine as they came into the kitchen. 'Do you like Eddie Eden?'

Laine made a face and shook her head.

'You don't?' Amanda said. 'Why not?'

'It's moronic,' Laine said. 'All that *la la la I love you* kind of stuff. Yuck! You'll see when you get older – you look for a lot more *meaning* in your music. My favourite band is Black Tulips. You won't have heard of them.'

'Uh . . . I think I have,' Amanda said.

'Well, I sure haven't,' I said.

'Of course *you* haven't,' Amanda said. 'You don't know anything about music. I think I heard their latest single on the radio. It was really good.'

Laine laughed. 'I doubt it, Amanda. They're a band of guys from college. They haven't made any records yet.'

'Oh!' Amanda said. 'Maybe I'm thinking of someone else. I'm sure they were called Black *somethings*.'

'Sure,' I said. 'I know who you're thinking of: Black *Fakers*!' I knew what Amanda was up to. She was desperate to impress Laine. Only, this time she'd flunked out.

Amanda stuck her tongue out at me.

'Do you have any orange juice?' Laine asked.

'Sure,' I said. 'Plenty. Watch out, though, or you'll step in—' Oops! Too late. Laine didn't watch where she was putting her feet. She put her heel right in Benjamin's food bowl.

'Yuck!' Laine exclaimed, lifting her foot out of the mush. 'What's that doing there?'

'Benjamin always has his dinner there,' I said. 'Sorry – I tried to warn you.'

'You feed it in the kitchen?' Laine said. 'What about hygiene?'

'Cats are really clean,' I said. 'Mom lets him eat in here.'

'Look,' Laine said, as she hopped over to the sink with her shoe in her hand and rinsed it under the tap. 'I'd really appreciate it if you didn't feed it in here.'

'But he always eats in here,' I said.

'He can eat out back for a few days,' Amanda said, picking up Benjamin's food and water bowls. 'I've always thought it was a bad idea to let him eat in the kitchen anyway.'

'Put them back!' I said. 'I'm not making Benjamin eat out in the yard. No way!'

Laine smiled at me. 'Please, Stacy? Just for me? I don't want to be difficult about this, but I really don't want it in here while I'm eating.'

I wished she would stop referring to Benjamin as *it*! It made him sound like he was a rock or something.

'Come on, Stacy,' Amanda said. 'It's no big deal. Mom said we should help Laine out any way we could.'

I guess she was right. I didn't want to start off our first day with Laine by having an argument with her over Benjamin.

'OK,' I said reluctantly. 'But I'm keeping his bowls right next to the door, OK?'

I wasn't happy about this, but I really didn't want to get on Laine's bad side. Especially not now I knew what she could be like if she got annoyed.

The difficult thing would be explaining to Benjamin why he suddenly had to have his meals out back. He wasn't going to like *that*, I can tell you. He wasn't going to like it one little bit.

Chapter Eight

MEMO.

From: *Benjamin Allen.*

To: *The President. American Association for the Prevention of Cruelty to Animals.*

Dear Sir/Madam,

I am writing to you to inform you of some recent developments in my home. I am, I would like to point out, a pedigree cat. I am a Russian Blue – I am not just some ordinary type of cat. I am a special cat, and deserve special treatment.

Up until now my human, Stacy Allen, has been treating me according to the guidelines set down in the Treatment of Special Cats manual. Paragraph five states: Your cat will be fed on demand in the kitchen. Your cat will be given a <u>bowl</u> for dry food, a bowl for gourmet canned food and a bowl of fresh water (which will be renewed frequently).

Imagine my shock when I discovered that

my food bowls had been dumped out in the yard without any explanation.

Imagine, also, the shock of being awoken from a sleep by having some strange person yelling at me. This is in clear violation of the Catnap sub-clause in paragraph seven.

It is bad enough that my owner's sister is constantly giving me a hard time, but there is now a new human making life almost impossible for me.

I look forward to the arrival of an inspector at my home at the earliest possible time. This situation must not be allowed to continue!

Yours sincerely,
Benjamin Allen. (Pedigree Russian Blue)

★   ★   ★

'It's only for a few days,' I told Benjamin later that night. I could tell he was mad at me. He was lying all bunched up at the foot of my bed with his tail toward me. He didn't even look around when I petted him.

'Look,' I said, 'it's not just you. I missed my favourite TV show tonight because Laine wanted to watch something on another channel.'

Laine hadn't just changed channels without asking, but she'd made it pretty clear that there was something else on that she wanted to see. And, of course, Amanda had backed her up.

Good old Amanda, always loyal to her little sister.

'We don't want to watch this junk,' she'd said, as soon as Laine had made it obvious that *she* didn't want to watch it.

'We *always* watch *Spindrift*,' I'd said. (*Spindrift* is my favourite soap – it's really fast-moving, and if you miss an episode it can take a couple of *weeks* to catch up.)

'*I* don't always watch it,' Amanda had said, using her really irritating grown-up voice. 'I only watch it to humour *you*, Stacy.'

Sheesh! What a liar! It's amazing her nose didn't start *growing* right then and there.

Anyway, we ended up watching something else. Something that Laine wanted to see, and something that Amanda *pretended* she wanted to see.

Mom called around bedtime to check that everything was OK.

I didn't complain about Benjamin's bowls being put out the back – I just kind of *mentioned* it in passing. I thought Mom would say I should bring them back into the house. But she didn't. She said it wouldn't hurt Benjamin to eat on the patio for a few days. Oh, yeah?

It's a shame Benjamin can't speak, or he would have told her exactly what he thought about *that*!

★ ★ ★

The next morning my cat alarm went off at the usual time.

Stacy! Breakfast time! Come on, Stacy, get moving. I'm hungry! Purrrr, purrrr, and a cold nose shoved in my ear.

I fixed Benjamin's breakfast and sat out on the patio with him while he ate it.

'Laine will get used to you,' I told him. 'You'll see. She'll love you just the same as I do once she gets to know you.'

I went back into the kitchen and got the breakfast stuff together. I put some coffee on for Laine and dropped a couple of Pop-Tarts in the toaster.

Amanda came wandering in, wearing her bathrobe and yawning.

'Do you want cereal or what?' I asked her.

'Nothing,' Amanda said.

'Huh?'

'I don't eat breakfast any more,' Amanda said.

I stared at her. Amanda usually eats enough

for ten starving lions first thing in the morning.

She looked at me. 'What's with you?' she said.

'Why don't you want breakfast?' I asked.

She shrugged. 'I just don't feel like it, that's all. Do you have a problem with that?'

'Not me,' I said. 'You will be the one fainting from hunger by ten o'clock.' I looked at her. 'You know, you don't have to do *everything* Laine does.'

'I don't know what you're talking about,' Amanda said.

'What's that mark on your leg?' I asked her. Just under the hem of her bathrobe I could see a small red line on her shin.

'Nothing,' Amanda said.

'It's a cut,' I said, looking closer. Amanda tried to hide her leg under the table. 'You shaved your legs!' I said.

'Hairy legs are gross,' Amanda said.

I just yelled with laughter.

'Quit laughing!' Amanda snapped.

'Do you want a band-aid?' I asked.

'No, I don't,' Amanda growled. 'And don't you dare tell Laine I used her razor.'

'It's not going to work,' I told her. 'You can

skip breakfast and shave your legs all you like, Amanda, but you still won't be eighteen.'

'I don't have the faintest idea what you're talking about,' Amanda said airily.

'Sure you don't,' I said.

I started on my breakfast. I could see Amanda watching every mouthful.

'Hungry?' I asked.

'Nope.'

'So why is your stomach rumbling?' I asked. I could hear it clear across the table. *Grrowwlll, grrumble, grrroan.*

'Hi, guys,' Laine said, coming fully dressed into the kitchen. She was in jeans and a sweater, but she still managed to look like she'd stepped right off the cover of a fashion magazine. And her hair was kind of swept up and back in this real neat style, held in place by a pair of clips.

Amanda just gazed at her in total envy.

'I've made some coffee for you,' I told Laine.

'Great,' she said. 'I can never get started in the morning until I've had at least two cups of coffee.'

'I'll just go get dressed,' Amanda said.

Laine smiled. 'And you can show me your

room, if you like,' she said. 'I'd like to see all your art stuff, Amanda.'

Wow – this was a change of behaviour! Maybe I'd misjudged Laine. Maybe she had just been feeling tired and ratty yesterday.

'Oh,' Amanda said, sounding a little edgy. 'Sure, I'll just go and clean up. My room's a little messy.'

I nearly choked on my Pop-Tart.

'A little messy?' I said. 'You've got to be kidding!'

Have you heard of the Twelve Labours of Hercules? (Hercules was this ancient Greek hero who was given twelve impossible tasks to do.) Well, meet the Thirteenth Labour of Hercules: cleaning Amanda's bedroom.

'Yes,' Amanda said. 'A *little* messy.' She smiled at Laine. 'It will only take five minutes.' She rushed upstairs.

'If she's really going to clean her room,' I said to Laine, 'we won't see her again until Friday.'

Laine sat down with a cup of coffee.

'What are your plans for today, Stacy?' she asked.

'I hadn't really thought about it,' I said. Then I had an idea. I told Laine about the accident with Mom's vase. After all, if Laine was in a better mood now, she might feel like helping us out.

'Would you come to the mall with us?' I asked. 'We went there last week, but we couldn't decide on what to buy. Maybe you could help?'

'I guess so,' Laine said. 'I'd kind of planned on a quiet day in front of the TV, but I suppose I could come along to the mall.'

'Don't you have any places you want to visit during the week?' I asked her.

Laine yawned. 'Not really,' she said. 'I just want to have a rest. You and Amanda can go out as much as you like – don't worry about me. I can keep myself amused.'

'I thought we'd do things together,' I said. 'All three of us.'

Laine gave a pretty unconvincing smile. 'Why not?' she said.

I'd noticed that 'why not?' was about as enthusiastic as she got about anything these days. College must be a lot more tiring than I'd imagined. I was beginning to wonder if the cousin Laine I had in my mind was someone *else*.

'Do you want to take a look at *my* room?' I asked.

'Sure,' Laine said.

I took Laine up to my room. From the next room I could hear Amanda clattering around in her cleaning frenzy. I showed Laine my books and my collection of pigs and frogs.

I was explaining where I'd gotten my favourite frogs from when Amanda came barging in with a big roll of pieces of paper under her arm.

'Ready,' she said to Laine. 'Come and see.'

As Laine walked out, Amanda shoved the roll of paper stuff in my hands.

'Dump this for me, Stacy,' she said. *Oh, right – call me Stacy the garbage collector.* The roll came unwound in my hands and I saw the top half of Eddie Eden's face staring up at me. Before I had a chance to say anything, Amanda had dragged Laine out and down the hall.

I dropped the roll on the floor in my room and went to see what Amanda had been doing.

Do you want to know what she'd done? She sure hadn't tidied up much. The only difference I could see was that every single picture of Eddie Eden had been taken down.

That's what she'd shoved into my hands. Every trace of her ever having adored and drooled over Eddie Eden was gone. And all because Laine had said she didn't like him.

I mean, come on – was my sister cracking up, or what?

Chapter Nine

Was there any end to what Amanda would do to try and be like Laine? I could see it all now.

'Do you know what I really like to do?' Laine would say. 'I like to put on flippers, a tutu and a fireman's helmet and perch on rooftops whistling like a bird.'

Five minutes later, there's this strange noise from outside the house. I go to check it out, and what do I see? You've got it – Amanda is sitting up on the roof in flippers, a tutu and a fireman's helmet, whistling away like a totally mad bird.

Well – it wasn't *quite* that bad, but the way Amanda was behaving it was only a matter of time. I mean, I still *like* Laine, I really do. Apart from her *cat* problem, and the fact that she seems to find it a major effort to *do* anything, and the way she flared up over that sweater, she's a really great person – but that doesn't mean I want to copy everything she does.

Laine had been in the house for one day, and already Amanda was doing her best to turn herself into a mini version of her. Laine Junior!

What next?

Laine was upstairs getting ready for our trip to the mall when I went into the kitchen. Hmm, interesting sight. The refrigerator door was open and Amanda's rear end was sticking out.

'What are you doing?' I asked.

'Ow!' Amanda said as her head hit a shelf in the refrigerator. She gave me a guilty look around the side of the door. Her cheeks were bulging with food. She chewed and swallowed.

'Nothing,' she said.

'You're not fooling anyone,' I told her as she wiped her hand across her mouth and slammed the refrigerator door closed. 'I knew you wouldn't be able to last without any breakfast.'

'I wasn't eating,' Amanda said. 'I was just checking that the pasta salad wasn't going bad.'

I pulled the refrigerator door open. The tub

of salad was almost empty – and we'd only eaten about a third of it the night before. Amanda must have wolfed the rest.

'Pasta salad?' I said. 'For *breakfast*?'

'I don't *eat* breakfast,' Amanda said. 'I told you, I was just checking it.'

'That was some check!' I said. 'Do you want to eat the rest, just to make sure? Look, there's some ham you've missed. And salami. And by the way, what am I supposed to do with all those pictures of your heartthrob Eddie Eden?'

Amanda shrugged. 'Do whatever you want with them. I don't want them any more. And you can have the CD and tapes as well. I dumped them on your bed.'

Boy, when Amanda sets out to impress someone, she sure goes all the way. Still, if Amanda was throwing Eddie Eden tapes and CDs out, I was perfectly happy to have them. I wasn't crazy about him the way Amanda had been before Laine appeared, but the music was OK. And if Amanda continued to act like this, I could do really well out of this week.

* * *

The three of us headed for the china shop in the mall. Luckily, the woman assistant who had been following us around on our last visit wasn't there, so we didn't have to keep pretending we were rich.

'What kind of thing are you looking for?' Laine asked.

'Just something nice for the living room,' Amanda said.

'I like this one,' I said, pointing to the vase I'd seen last time – the yellow one with the sunflowers all around it.

Amanda opened her mouth to say something, but before she had the chance to say a word, Laine had picked the vase off the shelf.

'So do I,' Laine said. 'It's real pretty.' She looked at the price tag underneath. 'And it's not too expensive, either.'

Amanda was standing there looking as if she'd just swallowed her tongue. Laine agreed with me! Whoo! Chew on *that*, Amanda!

'That was the one I liked best,' Amanda said.

'You did not!' I said. 'You hated it. You said it was the wrong colour and everything.'

Amanda shook her head. 'No way,' she said. 'You're thinking of some other vase, Stacy. This was the one I wanted to buy all along.'

Well, do you like *that*! Amanda was lucky I didn't bounce that vase off her *head*! And the only reason I didn't was because I didn't want to go crazy in front of Laine.

Anyway, we bought the vase and the saleswoman gift-wrapped it for us.

We spent the rest of the morning wandering around the mall and then had lunch at McDonald's.

'I'm really glad you came to stay with us,' Amanda said to Laine. 'We can do lots of things together.'

Laine nodded. 'Yeah,' she said. 'Maybe I can think of somewhere special where we can go.' She smiled. 'A nice surprise.'

'When?' Amanda asked. 'Where?'

'That'll be part of the surprise,' Laine said.

We finished eating.

'I think I'll just go for a look around on my own,' Laine said. 'I'll see you back at the house.'

I watched Laine walk off.

'I sometimes think she doesn't really want to *be* with us,' I told Amanda.

'What do you mean?' Amanda asked. 'Of course she wants to be with us. Otherwise she wouldn't have come to look after us.'

'I don't know,' I said, shaking my head. 'She's changed an awful lot.'

'It's called growing up,' Amanda said.

'Something you wouldn't know anything about.'

'Well,' I said, 'if *that's* growing up, you can keep it. She was a whole lot nicer when she was younger.'

'You're just annoyed because she doesn't like that cat of yours,' Amanda said. '*I* can't see anything wrong with her at all. And now, if you don't mind. I think I'll take a walk around – on my *own*!'

She marched off with her nose in the air. This was getting so weird. Amanda was watching every move Laine made, and doing her best to copy her. And she was falling over herself to agree with every single thing Laine said.

What do I have here? A sister or a parrot?

The Stacy Allen Book of Rare Birds

The Blonde-crested, Loud-beaked Amanda Bird

This North American bird is noted for its big head, colourful plumage and loud, repetitive call. Also known as the 'Yeah, Laine' bird, it will quickly learn to mimic the behaviour of other, older birds, and can be seen in its natural habitat, hopping from foot to foot and repeating the phrases 'Yeah, Laine, I agree with you,' and 'Yeah, Laine, I think so, too,' until it drives every other bird within earshot crazy.

It also has the unpleasant habit of putting down smaller birds of its own species, although if it's not *very* careful it may find itself getting very severely *pecked*!

I made my own way home. Laine was lying on the couch in the living room, glued to the telephone. I gave her a wave from the hall. She waved back and kicked the door shut.

I was a little offended, I can tell you. As if I'd listen in on her phone calls!

Laine Shelby Baxendale – you are *not* the cousin that I remember!

I went into the kitchen and took a yoghurt out of the refrigerator.

'Sorry about that,' Laine said, coming into the kitchen a few minutes later. 'It was kind of private. I was talking to Matt.'

'No problem,' I said. 'Did you run into Amanda again in the mall?'

'No, but she's home now,' Laine said. 'I heard her upstairs.'

I gave her a thoughtful look. 'It was nice of

you to agree to come and look after us,' I said. 'I'm sure you've got plenty of things you'd rather be doing.'

'Not at all,' Laine said with a smile. 'It's a pleasure.'

'Really?' I said. I hoped she meant that. I was still willing to give her the benefit of the doubt.

'Sure,' Laine said.

I smiled. 'Do you want to come to the swimming pool with us this afternoon?'

'Yeah, OK,' said Laine.

'Great!' I said. 'I'll go and tell Amanda.'

Amanda wasn't in her room. But then I saw that the door to Laine's room was ajar, and I heard a voice from inside.

'Oh, hi,' I heard. 'My name? I'm Amanda Allen. Well, my full name is Amanda Laine Allen. What's your name? Kurt? Well, hi, Kurt, nice to meet you.'

What was Amanda up to? It sounded like she was on the phone. I crept over to the slightly open door.

'Well, how old do you *think* I am?' Amanda said in a real cutesy kind of voice. 'Eighteen?' She gave a little laugh. 'Well, I'm not *quite* eighteen yet, but everyone says I could pass for eighteen. What kind of music do I like?

96

My favourite group is Black Orchids, but you probably never heard of them. They're new, you know, but they're going to be really big one day. Yeah, that's right, I like to keep up with the latest things, you know?'

I peeped through the gap. Amanda was sitting at Mom's dressing table, looking at herself in the mirror. She'd put on some of Laine's make-up and had her hair clipped back so that it was something like Laine's hairstyle – only not as good.

'You think I've got a nice figure?' she said with a giggle. Her lips were covered with bright red lipstick. 'Well, thank you. I do like to keep myself in shape. I work out every single day. Huh? Yeah, sure, I'd love to have dinner with you one night. Gee, I don't know if I can make it tonight – I have such a busy social life. Tomorrow night? Sure, that'll be great. I'll look forward to it, Kurt.'

I didn't know what to do. It was pretty embarrassing, catching her fantasizing to herself in the mirror. I thought maybe it would be kinder just to creep away, but I have to admit, I couldn't resist letting her know she'd been caught at it. Sure, it's not very *kind*, but I'm only *human*, and this was a golden opportunity to score against Amanda.

I coughed loudly and pushed the door open.

Amanda nearly jumped clean off the stool, and the lipstick she'd been waving around went flying across the room.

'Stacy!' she yelled. 'Don't *do* that!'

I went into the room. 'Does Laine know you're using her stuff?' I asked.

'She won't mind,' Amanda said. 'Just don't tell her, OK? And you shouldn't just barge in on me like that. I could have been doing something private.'

I looked at her. 'I know you don't take much notice of anything I say,' I said, 'but you don't look eighteen.'

Amanda shrugged. 'Who says I want to look eighteen?' she said. 'Anyway, Laine said I looked fifteen – and that was without make-up on. I'm going to ask Laine to do a real make-over on me. Then you'll see!'

'And how's she going to make it so you *act* eighteen?' I asked.

'I already do,' Amanda said. 'You're just jealous, Stacy, because Laine and I have so much in common, and you're too young to understand.'

'Get out of here!' I said. 'Compared to Laine, you're just a kid. Oh – and Laine's favourite group isn't Black Orchids – it's Black

Tulips. At least you could try to get *that* right before you start showing off in front of non-existent boys.'

Amanda's cheeks went bright red. She got up and pushed past me out of the room.

'I'm sorry,' I said. 'I didn't mean it. Amanda?'

She slammed into the bathroom. I'd really upset and embarrassed her. But sometimes she gets me so mad!

'Amanda?' I called, tapping at the bathroom door. 'We're going swimming this afternoon. Are you coming with us? I'm sorry about what I said. I didn't mean to upset you. Amanda? Hey – Amanda? I bet you'll pass for eighteen with make-up on.'

The door opened and Amanda glared at me.

'That's right, I would,' she said. 'And do you know what you'd pass for in full make-up? You'd pass for a *clown*!'

She slammed the door.

Oh, well. I guess I deserved that.

Chapter Ten

It was Wednesday morning. Laine was having a shower, so I took the opportunity to bring Benjamin's food bowls back into the kitchen. I was sitting on the floor with him while he ate. He was pleased to be eating indoors again. Benjamin can purr and eat at the same time, and he was really enjoying his food.

Amanda came into the kitchen. 'He shouldn't be in here,' she said.

'Laine isn't going to know,' I said. 'Not unless some *sneak* tells her. Do you know any sneaks who might tell her, Amanda?'

Amanda went straight to the cookie jar. She'd skipped breakfast again, but I guess she was too hungry to pretend in front of me any more.

'I think Laine is planning on taking me to the disco this evening,' Amanda said.

'Says who?' I said. 'What disco?'

'I saw the tickets in her room,' Amanda said, as she wolfed down a cookie. 'For Sparkles.'

Sparkles is a disco in town. I didn't know much about it – but I did know one thing: you had to be sixteen to get in. 'She must have bought them when she went off on her own the other day in the mall.'

'What were you doing nosing around in her room?' I asked.

'I was just looking at her things,' Amanda said. 'I wasn't prying.'

'So what makes you think she'd take you to Sparkles?' I said.

'Who else is there?' Amanda said. 'She said she'd take us somewhere special. Remember? When we were in McDonald's? *This* must be what she had in mind. A surprise trip to Sparkles!'

'Hang on,' I said. 'We're not *sixteen*! We'd never get in.'

'I can pass for sixteen,' Amanda said. 'At least, I will once Laine's done a make-over on me. And there were only *two* tickets, Stacy. I don't think you're coming with us. There's no way you could ever look sixteen.'

'Have you asked Laine about this?' I said.

'No, of course not,' Amanda said. 'I don't want her to know I've been in her room. And you're not going to say anything, either, OK? She obviously wants it to be a surprise.'

'I'll have plenty to say if you get taken to a disco and I get left at home!' I said.

'Maybe she'll plan something else for you,' Amanda said. 'Something more for kids your age.'

Amanda took a handful of cookies and walked out. 'And you'd better put that cat's bowls outside before Laine sees them,' she called back. 'Or else you'll get in trouble.'

'He's called *Benjamin*!' I yelled after her. Benjamin stared at me. 'Don't worry,' I told him, giving him a stroke, 'things will be back to normal soon.'

★　★　★

It was lunchtime and I was looking through Mom's list of frozen meals to see what to take out for dinner, when Amanda came running in.

'Where's Laine?' she asked.

'She's locked herself in the living room with the telephone,' I told her. 'Have you asked her about Sparkles yet?'

'Shh!' Amanda said. 'I'm not supposed to know about it.'

'Look,' I said. 'If Laine *was* planning on

taking you out, don't you think she'd have said something by now?'

'Not if it was a *surprise*,' Amanda insisted. 'She's saving it for the last minute.'

'And what's *my* surprise?' I said.

Amanda was about to say something back when we heard Laine come out of the living room.

'Don't say a word!' Amanda hissed. She turned and gave Laine a big smile as she came into the kitchen. 'Hi,' Amanda said, smiling from ear to ear and kind of wriggling with barely hidden excitement. 'Remember you promised me a make-over? I thought maybe this afternoon would be a good time?'

'Yeah, OK,' Laine said. 'We could do it now, if you want.'

'Yes, please,' Amanda said.

'OK,' Laine said. 'You go on up. I'll be with you in a minute.'

Amanda went racing up the stairs as if she was running on hot coals.

Laine smiled at me. 'You don't mind, do you?' she asked. 'I know Amanda really wants me to make her over. I could probably do you too, if you like.'

'No, that's OK,' I said. I looked at her. 'Do you have anything planned for today?' I asked her as casually as I could. 'For *later* today, I mean?'

Laine smiled. 'I hope so,' she said. 'If I can arrange everything.' She smiled. 'I'd better go get to work on Amanda. These things take time, you know.'

'Can I watch?' I asked. 'While you do Amanda?'

'Sure,' she said. 'Why not?'

* * *

'Well?' Laine asked. 'Is madame satisfied?'

Amanda stared at her new self in the mirror. It was pretty amazing. An hour ago Amanda had sat down there looking like a pretty thirteen-year-old. But *now*! Now she looked like a real teenager.

Laine had styled her hair in a different way. She'd worked on Amanda with brushes and make-up until Amanda looked like she was a fashion model.

I had to admit it – Amanda would easily pass for sixteen.

'It's fabulous,' Amanda said, staring at herself. 'At last I look as grown up as I feel. Oh, Laine – it's wonderful!'

'How old do you think you could make *me*

look?' I asked Laine. 'If you did the same to me?'

She smiled. 'I guess we could add a couple of years,' she said.

Oh, great! Amanda gets made up and looks at least sixteen. I get made up and look *twelve*!

Laine smiled. 'Yup,' she said. 'I've got to admit. I did a good job there. What do you think, Stacy?'

'I'm impressed,' I said. 'But do you really have to spend *that* long every time you want to look good?' When *I* go somewhere special, all I have to do is pick something nice to wear, wash, brush my hair and I'm ready. I can't imagine spending an hour just on my *face*.

'It's worth the trouble,' Laine said, with a smile.

'It is?' I said. I wasn't so sure.

* * *

I was in my room a little later, doing some thinking.

If Laine was taking Amanda to Sparkles that evening, what was *I* supposed to do? Laine couldn't just leave me on my own. And if the trip to Sparkles was Amanda's special treat, where was mine?

That was when I heard voices through my

open window. Laine was talking over the back fence with Mrs Lloyd from next door. I didn't catch all they said, but I did hear *one* thing.

I heard Mrs Lloyd say, 'That's fine, Laine, leave it to me. I'll come over around seven-thirty.'

It didn't take a genius to figure out what *that* was all about. Laine had fixed it with Mrs Lloyd to come over and baby-sit for me.

Great, huh? Amanda gets swept off to Sparkles, looking like a fairy princess, and I get left with Mrs Lloyd.

Meet Cinderella Allen, the girl who doesn't get to go to the ball. And I'll tell you one thing – Mrs Lloyd might be a nice person, but she's no fairy godmother!

Chapter Eleven

Who wants to go to a disco anyway? I know what goes on in those places. Hundreds of people jumping around like salmon at spawning time. Who needs it? And the music is so loud in there that you can't even *talk* to anyone. I'd rather spend an evening in a clothes drier. I'd rather spend an evening in front of the TV. At least with Laine and Laine Junior out, I'd be able to watch my own TV shows.

I went into Amanda's room. There were clothes all over the bed and she was posing in front of the mirror in one of her best outfits.

'What do you think?' she asked.

'It looks fine,' I said, with a sigh.

She stopped preening herself and looked at me.

'Look,' she said. 'Laine couldn't take you. No one's going to believe you're sixteen, Stacy.'

'I know,' I said. 'You don't have to keep telling me. And I heard Laine arranging with Mrs Lloyd for her to come over. Sometimes I hate being ten.'

'Hey, cheer up, Stacy,' Amanda said. 'I'll tell you all about it when I get back. I'll tell you every detail – it'll be just like you were there.'

'Discos are too noisy, anyhow,' I said.

'That's right,' Amanda said. 'You probably wouldn't have enjoyed it.'

'I would!' I said. 'It's not fair! Why is Laine taking you somewhere I can't go? I bet Mom wouldn't be too happy if I told her! I bet Mom wouldn't let you go!'

'Stacy!' Amanda said, looking really shocked. 'You're not going to tell her?'

'Of course not,' I said. 'But I don't like being left out like this! I feel like telling Laine exactly what I think of her!' The more I thought about it, the madder I got.

'I'm sure Laine will make it up to you,' Amanda said. 'She must have something planned for you later in the week.'

'She'd better!' I said. 'And it had better be as good as being taken to Sparkles, that's all I can say! And I hope you get left with Mrs Lloyd while Laine and I are doing it.'

'Mrs Lloyd's not so bad,' Amanda said.

'I know,' I said. Actually, Mrs Lloyd is an OK baby-sitter, although she's a little set in her ways and doesn't like it if we're too loud. She's in her fifties, and she's short and round like a beach-ball, with grey hair and a lot of laugh-wrinkles on her face. I looked at Amanda. 'Are you wearing that?'

'I don't know,' Amanda said. 'I can't make my mind up.'

'You'd look better in that blue dress,' I said. 'You know – the one with the skinny shoulder-straps. It's more grown-up.'

'Do you think so?' Amanda said. 'I'll try it on. You tell me if it looks OK.'

She looked great in the dress. I could see how excited she was about being taken to Sparkles, and I didn't want to spoil it for her by being a pain. Am I a considerate sister, or what?

'Did Laine say what time you'll be leaving?' I asked her.

'She hasn't said anything at all,' Amanda said, twirling around in her dress. 'But she'll be in here any minute. And she'll say, *Hey, Amanda, have I got a surprise for you*! And I'll say, *What kind of surprise*? And she'll say, *I'm taking you to your first grown-up disco*!' Amanda's eyes shone. 'Stacy, it's going to be *great*!'

'You behave yourself, OK?' I said, imitating Mom's voice. 'I don't want to have to bail you out of a police cell.'

Amanda laughed. 'Do you know what I'm going to do?' she said. 'I'm going to call Cheryl. She'll be so jealous!'

Amanda shot down the stairs, leaving me sitting on her bed feeling like Cinderella all over again.

Stacyella

Act Two, Scene One
Stacyella sits sighing on her sister's bed with only her faithful cat for company.
Stacyella: Oh, kitty, I do wish I could go to the disco. (*Sigh*) But I fear such pleasures are not for the likes of me. (*Sigh*) I shall just have to stay behind and do my chores. (*Sigh!*) But at least I shall have you for company, my faithful feline friend.
There is a sudden flash of light and a little old lady in a big white dress appears out of nowhere. She spins around twice, waving a magic wand, and plops down on the carpet.

110

Fairy Godmother: Ohh! Those magic journeys always make me dizzy!

The Fairy Godmother climbs to her feet, shakes her dress out and looks at Stacyella and Benjamin the Cat, who are sitting with their mouths hanging open.

Stacyella [cheerfully]: Are you a fairy god-mother?

Fairy Godmother: I sure am, honey.

Stacyella: Have you come to take me to the disco after all? What do you need? Let me think. Four white mice for horses. A pumpkin for the coach. And Benjamin can be my foot-man! Oh, Fairy Godmother, may I really go to the disco?

The Fairy Godmother scratches her nose with the end of her wand.

Fairy Godmother: Which one of you is Benjamin?

Stacyella [puzzled – pointing to the cat]: He is. Do you want me to stand up so you can turn my old rags into a beautiful dress?

Fairy Godmother [ignoring Stacyella and waving her magic wand over the cat]: You *shall* go to the disco, Benjamin!

There is another flash of light and Stacyella turns to see Benjamin standing there dressed up and looking ready to dance the night away.

Stacyella: Excuse me, I think you've got the wrong person, Fairy Godmother.
Fairy Godmother: Nope. I don't think so. Come on. Benjamin, your carriage awaits. Oh, and Stacyella – get your chores done, huh? This place is a *mess*!
Exit Fairy Godmother and Benjamin in another flash.
Stacyella: Hey! Wait a minute! This can't be right! Get back here! Hey! Heyyyy!

I went out into the hallway just as Laine was coming out of her room. She was made up to kill and had this really slinky black dress on.

'Hi, Stacy,' she said. 'Where's Amanda? There's something I want to tell you both.'

'It's OK,' I said. 'I already know. You're going to the disco.'

Laine looked at me in surprise. 'How did you know that?'

'Amanda saw the tickets in your room, and I heard you talking to Mrs Lloyd,' I said. 'We kind of *guessed* the rest.'

Laine put her arms around me. 'I hope you don't mind,' she said. 'It's only for one night. *Do* you mind?'

'No,' I said bravely. 'You go and enjoy yourselves. I'll be OK.'

'I'll take you to the movies tomorrow night to make up for it,' Laine said with a smile. 'And you can have all the popcorn and ice-cream you can eat. How's that?'

'Do I get to pick the movie?' I asked.

'Sure,' Laine said.

'I wish I could come to the disco with you,' I said.

'You're not old enough,' Laine said.

'Yeah, well neither is Amanda,' I pointed out.

Laine looked at her watch. 'Matt should be here soon,' she said.

I looked at her. 'Matt?'

'You remember me mentioning him, don't you?' Laine asked. 'My boyfriend from college? He's driving over here tonight.'

Oh, great! Not only does Amanda get to go to the disco, but she gets driven there in Laine's boyfriend's car!

Amanda was just putting the phone down as we came down the stairs. She was grinning like an open piano. You can bet she'd called *all* her friends to tell them about the disco.

'That's a pretty dress,' Laine said.

'Do you think so?' Amanda said. 'It took me for ever to figure out what to wear.' She looked expectantly at Laine. 'You look great, too,' she said.

'Thank you,' Laine said. 'Stacy tells me you've already worked out what's happening tonight.'

'I sure have,' Amanda said with an even bigger grin. (Another half-inch of *grin* and the top of her head was going to fall right off.) 'I'm really looking forward to it.'

Laine gave her a puzzled look, but before anyone could say anything, there was the sound of a car horn beeping from outside.

'Matt!' Laine said, running to the front door.

'Matt?' Amanda said, looking at me.

I nodded. 'Matt is going, too. It looks like it'll be a threesome.'

We watched as Laine ran down the driveway. Matt was just getting out of his car. He was incredibly tall, and good-looking. The two of them kissed and walked arm in arm back up to the house.

'Matt,' Laine said, 'these are my cousins, Stacy and Amanda. Stacy and Amanda, this is Matt Ross.'

Matt smiled and stuck his hand out for us to shake.

'Good to meet you,' he said. (He seemed an OK kind of guy from what I could see.)

'I'll just go get my bag,' Laine said. She ran upstairs.

'Uh . . . did you have a long drive?' I asked.

'Yeah. Around an hour,' Matt said. 'I'm staying with my folks in Aston.'

'I've never been to Sparkles,' Amanda said, looking at him with big, shining eyes. 'It's supposed to be a great place.'

'I hope so,' Matt said. 'Uh, how's your grandpa?'

'It's our grandmother who had the accident,' I said. 'Mom called last night and said she's doing OK.'

'Good,' Matt said. 'I'm glad to hear it.'

'Would you like something to drink while you're waiting?' I asked.

'I don't think so, thanks,' Matt said. He looked at Amanda. 'I thought Laine said you were only thirteen,' he said. 'You look a lot older.'

A face-splitting smile from Amanda. 'Laine did the make-up for me,' she said. 'I can do it myself,' she added hastily, 'but Laine is a little better at it than I am. I'll pass for sixteen, won't I?'

'Easily,' Matt said. 'Are you going somewhere special?'

Amanda stared at him. *Oops*, I thought, *Laine hasn't told him that Amanda's going with them.*

Before anyone had a chance to say anything else, Mrs Lloyd came across the front lawn.

'Hello, everyone,' she said. 'You must be Laine's friend, Matt. I'm Emma Lloyd. I'll be sitting for the girls while you and Laine have your night out.' She shook hands with Matt.

'You've got it wrong,' Amanda said. 'It's only Stacy you'll be sitting for.'

'Are you sure?' Mrs Lloyd said. 'I'm sure that Laine said—'

Laine came running down the stairs with her bag.

'Mrs Lloyd!' she said. 'You're just on time. Thanks for helping me out like this.'

'It's no trouble,' Mrs Lloyd said. 'You youngsters go out and enjoy yourselves. We'll be just fine.'

Laine smiled at Amanda and me. 'See you later, then,' she said. 'I won't be back before you go to bed, but I'll tell you all about it in the morning.' She swept past us and linked arms with Matt.

I glanced at Amanda. She was standing there looking kind of stunned. She looked as if someone had just thrown a bucket of ice water over her.

'Bye,' Laine called, as she and Matt headed for the car.

'Uh, bye,' I said.

Amanda didn't say a word.

Chapter Twelve

'Well, now,' Mrs Lloyd said, closing the front door, 'do you girls have any plans for this evening?' She looked at Amanda. 'You're looking very smart, dear,' she said. 'Like a real young lady!'

Amanda stared at the closed door. I'd seen Amanda upset, and I'd seen her mad, but I'd never seen her look so totally shocked before.

'Is something wrong, dear?' Mrs Lloyd asked.

'No,' Amanda said softly. 'There's nothing wrong.'

I followed Mrs Lloyd into the living room, glancing back at Amanda, who was still just standing there like a rabbit about to be run over.

'We could watch some TV, if you like,' Mrs Lloyd said. 'Or we could play a game. How would you like that? Monopoly or something like that?'

'I'll get the board,' I said. I was thinking how bad Amanda must be feeling.

'That's the idea,' Mrs Lloyd said, sitting on the couch. 'A nice game of Monopoly.'

I went back into the hall and stood in front of Amanda.

'Hey,' I said. 'Are you OK?'

'She never planned to take me,' Amanda said. She sounded real choked up.

'I guess not,' I said. I could see tears glistening in her eyes. 'Do you want to play Monopoly with us?'

Amanda gave a sob and the tears spilled down her cheeks. 'She never even *thought* about it!' she said.

I looked anxiously at her. 'You'll spoil your make-up,' I said. 'Come on, Amanda, it's not so bad.'

'It is!' Amanda said. It's—' But then her voice choked up completely and she just turned and ran up the stairs.

I caught up with her in the bathroom. She was leaning over the sink, scrubbing all the make-up off her face.

'Don't cry,' I said. 'You'll only get bloodshot eyes.' I was trying to cheer her up. It made me feel bad to see her like that.

'I'm not crying!' Amanda said.

Amanda slooshed water over her face and looked at me. 'I feel so stupid!' Amanda said. 'I really believed she was going to take me. I honestly did!'

'You couldn't have known she was planning to go with Matt,' I said.

'But she said she was going to take us somewhere *special*!' said Amanda.

'She is,' I said. 'She told me earlier. We're going to the movies tomorrow night. That's our special treat – a *movie*.' I smiled hopefully at her. 'I'll let you pick which one,' I said. 'Hey, come on, Amanda; why don't you come down and play Monopoly with us?' I smiled at her. 'I'll let you win.'

'I don't want to,' Amanda said. 'I'm going to stay in my room. I don't want to talk to anyone. I don't want to see anyone. I never want to see Laine again!'

'What should I tell Mrs Lloyd?' I asked.

'Whatever you like,' Amanda said. 'I don't care what you tell her.'

I turned at the bathroom door. 'Hey, Amanda,' I said. 'I'm so sorry.'

In the end I told Mrs Lloyd that Amanda was up in her room listening to some records.

'I guess teenagers like their own company,' Mrs Lloyd said as I set up the Monopoly board. 'I used to spend hours on my own in my room when I was Amanda's age.' She smiled. 'Do you want the top hat or the car?'

'The car,' I said. It was kind of difficult to concentrate on the game, knowing that Amanda was upstairs feeling so bad. But what could I do? I couldn't tell Mrs Lloyd what had happened without making Amanda feel even *worse*. The last thing she wanted was for anyone else to know how dumb she'd been.

I'd been pretty sure that Amanda's efforts to keep up with Laine were going to fail, but she didn't deserve to be humiliated like that. Poor Amanda. I felt *so* sorry for her.

★ ★ ★

We didn't see Amanda again that night.

It wasn't much of a challenge, playing Monopoly with Mrs Lloyd. She kept forgetting what properties she had, and I had to spend half the game reminding her to charge me rent. I didn't even bother cheating. (I cheat a little when I play with Mom and Dad and Amanda – but only because we *all* do. It's just part of the fun.)

We watched some TV after the game and Mrs Lloyd told me how pleased she'd been with the painting Amanda had done of their dog.

'Your sister's a very talented girl,' she told me. 'I guess she'll want to go to art school when she's older.'

'I guess so,' I said. 'But I think she's more interested in just *being* older, right now.'

Mrs Lloyd shook her head. 'You young people,' she said. 'Always wishing your lives away.' She smiled at me. 'What I wouldn't give to be your age again!'

It sure is strange. *I'd* like to be *Amanda*'s age. *Amanda* wants to be the same age as *Laine*. And *Mrs Lloyd* just wants to be a kid again. Isn't anyone happy to be their own age?

I went up to bed a little later than usual, and left Mrs Lloyd watching TV. I thought of looking in on Amanda, but there weren't any sounds from her room, so I decided not to. I guessed she'd probably cried herself to sleep.

Benjamin was already curled up on my bed. Poor Benjamin, too. Life wasn't treating him so well just then, either. What with having to eat out the back and being shooed away by Laine all the time, and having doors shut in his face.

He came and sat on my chest once I was in

bed, and I stroked him for ages, trying to cheer him up.

I couldn't sleep. I guess I was half-listening for Laine to come back. I'm like that. When Dad gets back late, I can never fall asleep until I know he's home.

It was about midnight, and I was still wide awake – and now I was thirsty as well. Benjamin was asleep, stretched over my legs, and making snuffling noises and twitching his paws.

Dad says that means he's dreaming. What do cats dream about? Chasing birds, I guess. I wonder if Benjamin ever catches any birds in his dreams? He sure never catches any when he's awake.

I slid my legs out from under him and crept off to the bathroom to get myself a drink of water. I could hear the TV downstairs.

I was just about to go back to bed, when I heard the sound of a car pull up at the front of our house. I went over to the window. It was Matt's car. And in the front seat Laine and Matt looked like they were having an argument.

Laine sure looked mad as she got out of the car and slammed the door. She started walking up to the house. Matt chased after her, but she just shook his hand off her arm.

He stood there in the driveway looking at her for a few moments, then went back to the car and drove away.

I couldn't help wondering what they'd argued about. Maybe Matt had started talking to another girl? I've seen that kind of thing on TV where a guy takes one girl to a club and then dances with a different girl. That *always* causes big explosions!

I switched the bathroom light off and zipped back to my room. I waited by the door, listening for the sound of Laine coming in.

It was only a couple of minutes before I heard our front door open. There was a whispered conversation between Laine and Mrs Lloyd.

'I'm glad you had a good time,' I heard Mrs Lloyd say. 'The girls haven't been any trouble.'

'Thanks again,' I heard Laine say as she closed the door.

I thought I'd better get into bed in case Laine came up to check on us, but then I heard Amanda's bedroom door open.

'Hey, are you still up?' Laine said.

'Did you have a nice time?' I heard Amanda say in a cold voice.

'Yes, it was fine,' Laine said. 'But shouldn't you be asleep, Amanda?'

'Oh, right,' Amanda said. 'Us little *kids* have to be in bed real early.'

'Is something wrong?' Laine asked.

'What could possibly be wrong?' Amanda said sarcastically. 'Just because you let me think you were taking me to the disco – just because you made me up so I looked old enough to get in there, and then didn't *take* me!'

'I never told you I was taking you to the disco,' Laine said. 'What put that idea in your head?'

'You said I looked like a real teenager!' Amanda said.

'Hold on a minute,' Laine said. 'There's a big difference between *looking* like you're a teenager and actually *being* one. You're only thirteen, Amanda. I couldn't have taken you to the disco even if I'd wanted to. They wouldn't have let you in.'

'You could have said I was old enough,' Amanda said angrily. 'You could have got me in if you'd wanted to.'

'Oh, right,' Laine said. 'And what would your mother have thought of me if I had? For heaven's sake, Amanda – grow up!'

'I am grown up!' Amanda yelled. 'I thought we were friends! I thought you really liked me!'

'I do,' Laine said. 'Of course I like you.'

'If you really liked me, you'd have taken me to the disco,' Amanda said. 'I put on my best dress and everything!'

'Now look,' Laine said. 'I'm sorry if you thought I was going to take you out. But you can't blame me for *you* having got it all wrong. There's no way I was going to take you to a place that you're too young to be allowed in. And if you were a little older, you'd understand that. But you're just a kid, Amanda. A nice kid, but still just a kid.'

'I am not!' Amanda yelled. 'Stop talking to me like I'm a *kid*! I *hate* it!'

'Now you're being childish,' Laine said. I could tell from the tone of her voice that she was getting annoyed. 'Why don't you just go to bed and calm down a little?'

'I don't want to calm down,' Amanda hollered. 'And I'm not going to bed just because *you* say so! I'll stay up all night if I feel like it. You shouldn't have come to stay if you're not prepared to look after us properly!'

'What's that supposed to mean?' Laine said.

'It means going out with your boyfriend,

when you should be looking after us!' Amanda yelled. Amanda was starting to get totally unreasonable. She was happy enough for Laine and her to go out and leave *me* behind, but it was a different matter when it was *Amanda* being left at home. But when Amanda gets mad, being reasonable doesn't come into it.

And I didn't think it was such a good idea for Amanda to mention Matt right then – although how was she supposed to know Laine had just had a big argument with him?

'Fine,' Laine said angrily. 'You do that. You know something, Amanda, the way you're behaving makes me wish I'd never agreed to come over here and look after you.'

'I wish you *hadn't*!' Amanda yelled.

'Well, tough luck, Amanda – because you're stuck with me for the rest of the week. And I'm not looking forward to it any more than you are. I don't want to be stuck here with a couple of stupid *kids*!'

I heard Amanda stomp across the hall and slam her bedroom door. And for once I thought Amanda had a good reason for stomping and slamming!

Stupid kids! That included *me*! Laine thought we were both stupid kids.

OK, Laine, I thought, now *we know where we stand! Things are going to be a little different around here from now on.*

Chapter Thirteen

The first thing I did the next morning was bring Benjamin's bowls in from the backyard and open up a can of his favourite food.

Then I made myself breakfast and sat at the kitchen table, waiting for Laine to *dare* to come down and complain about Benjamin eating indoors.

One word out of her, I was thinking, *just one word, and I'll tell her exactly what I think of her*!

I don't know whether I was just *mad* at Laine, or whether it was the feeling of disappointment that hurt more. I could understand Laine getting mad at Amanda, but it was that comment about stupid *kids* that had really hurt me. *Stupid kids* meant *me* as well, and that's what Laine thought we were!

Usually when something upsets me this much, the first thing I do is go and talk to Cindy about it. Cindy is always sympathetic and understanding. (That's why she's my best friend.) But Cindy was out of town.

I sat pushing my cereal around in the bowl. I didn't feel in the least bit hungry, even though I had this huge hollow feeling in my stomach. It wasn't the kind of hollowness that goes away when you eat. It was *worse* than that.

I heard someone come down the stairs. I saw Benjamin's ears prick up.

'You just stay there,' I told him. 'You're not being ordered out any more.'

But it wasn't Laine. It was Amanda. She was dressed already – which was unusual for that time in the morning.

'Hey, Amanda,' I said, going out into the hall. She was looking at the postcard from Dad that had come in the mail the day before.

'Hi,' she said. On the front of the card was a photo of the Statue of Liberty. On the back Dad had written: *Having a terrible time. Wish I wasn't here. See you all on Saturday. All my love, Dad.*

'I heard you and Laine arguing last night,' I said.

'Yeah,' Amanda said. 'I guess we know where we stand now.' She opened the front door.

'Are you going out?' I asked.

'Yup,' Amanda said.

'Where?'

'I'm going over to Cheryl's house,' Amanda said. 'I'll probably be out all day.'

'Don't you want some breakfast first?' I asked.

'Nope,' Amanda said. '*She* might come down – and I don't want to see her. I don't want to see her ever again!'

Amanda left and I went back into the kitchen. Benjamin was up on the table with his face in my cereal bowl. He knows perfectly well that he's not allowed on the table, but I figured he'd had enough grief for one week, so I just sat down with my chin in my fists and let him carry on eating. I didn't want the stuff anyway. He was welcome to it.

Once he'd eaten all he wanted, he sat down in the middle of the table and started washing himself. I love watching him do that. He's real fussy about keeping himself clean. And he always does it in the same order. Right paw first to clean the right-hand side of his face – and then the left paw for the other side. Cats are *so* perfect. How can anyone *not* love cats?

I heard Laine moving around upstairs. On the previous two mornings I'd put some coffee on for her (I was always up first to feed Benjamin), but this morning she could fix her own coffee! In fact, I'd decided, she could do *all* her own stuff from now on.

Benjamin heard her coming down the stairs. He jumped off the table and headed for the cat-flap. It looked like everyone in the house wanted to avoid Laine that morning.

'Hi, Stacy,' Laine said. 'Have you seen Amanda? She's not in her room.'

'She's gone out,' I said.

'Oh. Do you know if she'll be long? I wanted to have a word with her.' Laine gave me an apologetic smile. 'We had a little argument last night – I wanted to clear the air.'

'I know,' I said. 'I heard it.'

'Did we wake you up?' Laine asked. 'I'm sorry.'

'I wasn't asleep,' I said. I gave her a meaningful look. 'I heard *everything*. Including the part about *stupid kids*.'

Laine looked awkward. 'I didn't mean that,' she said. 'I was in a bad mood already, and I just lost my temper. That's why I wanted to talk to Amanda about it.'

'She said she'd be out all day,' I said. 'So I guess you're going to have to wait.'

Laine sat down. 'Honestly, Stacy – I didn't

realize Amanda thought I was going to take her out. I didn't upset her on purpose. I wouldn't do that. You believe me, don't you? I didn't mean those things I said to her.'

'Which things didn't you mean?' I asked. 'About her being childish, or about you not looking forward to spending the rest of the week with two stupid kids?'

'I didn't mean that,' Laine said. 'I was annoyed – we all say dumb things when we're angry, Stacy.'

It would have been easy for me to have made up with Laine right then. But if Amanda was still mad at her, then I certainly wasn't going to forgive Laine that easily. There are times when sisters have got to stick together – especially *stupid* sisters!

I got up from the table.

'Stacy,' Laine said. 'Let's talk about this. There's no need for us not to get along.' She tried to catch my arm as I walked past, but I shook her off.

'I'm going out, too,' I said. 'And I'll be out all day.' I walked out of the kitchen.

'Stacy! Come back here!' Laine called. 'Don't be silly.'

I ran up to my room to get a jacket. Laine was waiting for me at the foot of the stairs.

133

'Don't forget we're going to the movies tonight,' she said. 'Any movie you like, OK?'

'I don't want to go to the movies,' I said. 'I only like going to the movies with *friends*.' I walked past her and opened the front door. I gave her a hard look. 'And I don't count a person who thinks I'm a stupid kid as my friend.'

* * *

I caught a bus into town and wandered around the mall for a while. But I didn't really enjoy it – I was too upset and hurt to have any fun. I bought myself a candy bar and went to take a look in the pet store. It's called Pet Paradise and it sells all kinds of animals.

It's even got a vivarium with snakes and lizards in it. I'm not sure if I like the idea of people having lizards for pets. I'm sure lizards would rather be out in the desert where they're supposed to be. And it's not as if you can have a lot of fun with a pet *snake*. (Fern doesn't agree with me on this – she's always said she'd love to have a pet snake, only her parents won't let her. Fern's a little *strange* in some ways, if you ask me.)

The most spectacular thing they've got in Pet Paradise is a huge red macaw called

Tonton. From its beak to the end of its tail feathers, it must be about three feet long. It sits on a big old branch set in a bucket of gravel in the middle of the shop, cracking nuts and chattering away to itself. The storekeeper told me Tonton is worth over eight hundred dollars.

Even Benjamin didn't cost anything like that much. And what if you bought it and it flew away back to Africa, or wherever they come from?

No, I think I'll stick to cats.

The man at the store knows me, because that's where I buy toys and special treats for Benjamin. (I had a count up of Benjamin's toys the other day – Mom had been complaining about them being all over the house. Would you believe Benjamin has a grand total of seventeen toys?)

When I go in there, I always head straight for the cages where they keep the kittens. There were some really gorgeous little fluffy black-and-white kittens for sale. I put my finger through the grill and they all gathered around, making a little yipping, squeaking noises. You've got to be careful, though, with kittens, because they've got teeth like needles.

After I'd said hello to the kittens, I bought

Benjamin a new toy. It was a ball of yellow fur with plastic eyes and a big grin. It was on a piece of elastic so you could hang it from a doorknob or whatever and it would bounce around. Benjamin would just love that.

Spending some time in the pet store helped me to calm down a little. Being with animals always makes me feel better if I'm in a bad mood. I mean, animals don't let you down the way some *humans* do.

I still didn't feel like going home, though. I bought myself a burger for lunch and spent the afternoon in Maynard Park, watching the ducks on the pond there.

That gave me some time to think. Maybe I was being a little hard on Laine. After all, Amanda hadn't exactly been acting reasonably last night, and Laine really didn't mean to upset Amanda. And she *had* just had an argument with Matt . . . Maybe if I explained that to Amanda, we could all get back to being friends.

I decided that maybe I should give Laine a chance to make up with us. And it had been kind of childish of me, I guess, to say I didn't want to go to the movies – especially as I *did*. There was a film showing that week called *Out of the Wild*. It sounded really good. It was about a boy who finds out that some property developers want to build on land where a herd of deer live, and about what he does to try and stop them.

I caught the bus home. I was prepared to apologize to Laine about saying she wasn't my friend. At least, I *was* until I actually got home – I changed my mind pretty quickly then!

The living-room door was closed and I could hear that the TV was on in there.

'Benjamin!' I called. 'Mommy's home! Benjamin! I've got a new toy for you!'

There was no sign of him. I went into the kitchen. His food bowls were gone, but that wasn't the worst of it. *Someone* had put a chair up against the cat-flap. *Laine*, of course! The nerve of her – blocking the cat-flap so he couldn't get in!

I pulled the chair away and opened the back door.

'Benjamin!' I called. 'It's OK, you can come in now!' But he wasn't there. Boy, was I mad.

Laine must have heard me, because when I looked around, she was standing in the kitchen doorway with her arms folded.

'So you decided to come back,' she said.

'What have you done with Benjamin?' I yelled.

'Don't talk to me about that darned cat,' Laine said crossly. 'I shut him out – the pest!'

'You can't do that,' I said. 'He's got every right to be in here!'

'Not when I find him sleeping on my best cashmere sweater, he hasn't!' Laine said. 'It was totally covered in hairs.'

'He can't help that,' I said. 'He's moulting. You should keep your bedroom door shut!'

'I did,' Laine said. 'He must have sneaked in there without me seeing. So I chased him out and put a chair across the flap so he couldn't get back in. That cat is totally untrained.'

'He *is* trained,' I yelled. 'He's the best-trained cat in the world. When did you lock him out?'

'This morning,' Laine said.

'You mean, he's been locked out of the house all day?' I said. 'How could you!'

'Stacy, it's only a *cat*,' Laine said. 'And I put its food bowls out – it's not as if it's going to starve.'

'He's not an *it*!' I hollered. 'He's a *he*!' I ran out into the backyard, calling Benjamin's name and looking all around for him.

'Calm down, Stacy,' Laine said, following

me out. 'It'll come back. *He'll* come back, I mean.'

'We've got to look for him,' I said. 'He could be anywhere.'

'Get out of here,' Laine said. 'I'm not looking for him. He'll turn up when he feels like it.' She went back into the house.

Of all the unfeeling people! And to think I was just about to *forgive* her! If anything had happened to Benjamin I wouldn't forgive her for the rest of my life!

Chapter Fourteen

'Benjamin!' I ran over to the fence at the Lloyds' side. I didn't *think* he'd be in there, because of their dog. Whisky goes crazy if Benjamin so much as shows his nose in there. And then Benjamin will zip up on to a fence-post and just sit there watching in this really unconcerned way while Whisky barks like mad and jumps up at him.

The Lloyds have a small dog-flap in their back door, and as I leaned over the fence and called, the flap went *whacketty-whacketty* and Whisky came racing out, barking up a storm.

'I wasn't calling you,' I told him. 'I was calling Benjamin.' Whisky came over to the fence and did his pleased-to-see-you routine. Tail wagging, tongue lolling out, jumping up at the fence. I leaned right over and gave him a pat on the head. He scampered into the middle of the yard and then back to the fence, looking at me with his big eyes as if he hoped I'd go over there and play ball with him.

But I didn't have time to play with Whisky. I ran to the other side of the yard and called some more.

Food, I suddenly thought. Benjamin always comes if you rattle a food box.

I ran into the kitchen and grabbed a box of Gourmet Cat-Munchies out of the closet.

I stood out on the patio, shaking the box and yelling. I was getting really worried now. Benjamin hardly ever roams far from the house. But then Benjamin had never been shut out like that before.

I could imagine what had happened. First Laine had chased him out of the house, and then, when he tried to get back in, he found the cat-flap wouldn't open. So what would he do? He'd sit by the cat-flap for a while, I guessed, trying to figure out what was going on. But then what? Maybe he'd go round to the front of the house, and see if he could get in that way.

I ran round the house and stood in the driveway, calling and rattling the box.

I was still out there when I saw Amanda come around the corner.

'Amanda!' I yelled. 'Quick!'

She came running across the road. 'What is it?' she asked.

'Benjamin's missing!' I told her.

She rolled her eyes. 'Oh, for heaven's sake, Stacy,' she said. 'What's with the big panic? He's probably asleep in a closet somewhere.'

'No, he isn't!' I said. 'Laine chased him out and put a chair up against the cat-flap, so he couldn't get in. He's been locked out of the house *all day*! He could be anywhere!'

'OK, Stacy,' Amanda said. 'Calm down. He couldn't have gone far. Where have you looked?'

'Everywhere!' I said. There was a big lump in my throat and I could feel tears pricking in my eyes. 'I've looked everywhere!'

'No you haven't,' Amanda said. 'If you'd looked *everywhere*, you'd have found him.'

'Not if he's run away!' I wailed.

'Stacy! Don't panic,' Amanda said. 'I'll help you look for him. Where's Laine? Shouldn't she be out here looking, too?'

'She won't,' I said. 'She doesn't care.'

'We'll see about that,' Amanda said determinedly. She marched up to the front door and let herself in. I stayed outside, calling and shaking the box.

Half a minute later, Amanda came out again, looking real annoyed.

'You're right,' she said. 'She's not going to help. She thinks he'll come home by himself when he gets hungry.'

'I told you so,' I said.

'Yeah, well, forget about Laine,' Amanda said. 'Have you been to any of the neighbours' houses yet? You never now, he might be curled up on someone's couch.'

I hadn't thought of that.

'OK,' Amanda said, pointing to the left. 'I'll try this way, you go the other way.' She smiled reassuringly at me. 'Don't worry, Stacy. Benjamin knows how to look after himself. I'm telling you, he'll be snoozing on a rug somewhere with a saucer of milk in front of him. Trust me.'

Amanda was only trying to calm me down, but the thought of Benjamin preferring to live somewhere else didn't exactly make me feel better.

Amanda ran off to ring on the first doorbell. I went across to the Lloyds' house and rang. There was no reply. Mr and Mrs Lloyd must have gone out somewhere. I was sure they wouldn't mind if I took a quick look out back.

I closed their side gate behind me so Whisky couldn't get out.

Whisky came scampering up to me, barking and wriggling.

'Hello, boy,' I said, patting his side as he raced round and round my feet. 'Have you seen Benjamin? Has he been over here at all?'

I walked around to the garden with Whisky bounding around me. 'Benjamin!'

'Myowwwl!'

'Whisky! Quiet, boy!' I crouched down and grabbed hold of the wriggly little terrier. 'Benjamin!' I called again.

'Miroo. Mirowwwl.'

It was Benjamin. He sounded close by, but I couldn't see him anywhere. Then Whisky wriggled out of my hands and went racing over to a narrow little vent at the bottom of the back wall of the house. He started barking and whining, his front paws scrabbling at the vent.

I ran after him. The vent was open a little way. We had a vent just like that at the back of our house. It led into the basement.

'Benjamin?' I called, kneeling down and peering through the vent. 'Benjamin!' I saw a grey furry face staring out at me.

'Mowwl!'

I grabbed Whisky and pulled him away.

144

'Benjamin!' I gasped in relief. 'What the heck are you doing down there? Come on out this instant! I've nearly had a heart attack over you!' I held Whisky firmly in my arms. 'Come on, Benjie, it's OK. Mommy's here. You're perfectly safe.'

That's what *I* thought!

Just as Benjamin came slinking out through the vent, Whisky gave a really fierce wriggle and jumped clean out of my arms.

'Whisky! No!' I yelled. But it was too late. Benjamin took one look at Whisky and went streaking down the yard like his tail was on fire. The Lloyds have this really big tree at the end of their backyard. Benjamin took a flying leap at the tree, landing on it halfway up the trunk. For a second I thought he was going to fall straight off, but somehow he got himself up the rest of the trunk and disappeared up into the branches.

Whisky skidded up to the bottom of the tree and started jumping up, kicking up a real racket, trying to get at Benjamin.

I ran to the end of the backyard. 'Bad dog!' I said. 'You shouldn't chase him! Look what you've done!' I looked up the tree. I couldn't see so much as a whisker of Benjamin. The tree was about 25 feet high, and the lowest branches were at least two feet above my head.

I managed to get hold of Whisky's collar and tow him away from the tree. But there was no way Benjamin was going to come down while Whisky was still in the yard.

I did some quick thinking. The Lloyds have a rock garden under the tree. I picked up the biggest rock I could carry and carried it back to the house. Then I grabbed Whisky again and managed to shove him in through the dog-flap. Before he could come zooming out again, I dumped the rock up against the flap.

Rattle, rattle, went the flap. *Bark, bark, whine,* went Whisky – but he couldn't get out. Step One of Operation Rescue Benjamin was complete.

But Benjamin wouldn't come down from the tree, no matter how much I called to him and told him everything was OK.

I guess he was up there thinking, *First you lock me out of my house, and then you set a dog on me. No way am I coming down, buster! No way!*

Amanda would help. I ran to go and find her.

She was about four doors down. I told

her I'd found Benjamin and the two of us went back into the Lloyds' yard.

'Come down here, you big, dumb cat!' Amanda yelled up into the tree. 'Come down right now, or I'll skin you alive and use your fur for mittens!'

'Amanda!' I said. 'Don't say things like that.'

Amanda laughed. 'He doesn't understand English,' she said. 'He doesn't know what I'm saying, Stacy.'

'All the same,' I said. 'Don't *threaten* him like that. Be nice to him.' I rattled the food box again and called up to him.

'Coo-ee,' Amanda called sweetly. 'Coo-ee! Benjamin? I've got some lovely fishie-wishie down here for you. Yummy! Nice fresh fishie-wishies!' There was a rustle up in the tree and a mournful miaow. 'Benjamin!' Amanda hollered. 'If you don't come down *right now* you won't get any fishie-darned-wishies!'

'I don't think he *can* get down,' I said. 'That was his *help, I'm stuck* meow.'

'Oh, great,' Amanda said. 'What do we do now? Call the fire department?'

'Couldn't you climb up?' I said.

'You must be joking,' Amanda said. 'I'll tell

you what. I'll give you a leg-up. You go and get him.'

'I can't,' I said. 'You know I hate heights. *I'll* get stuck up there, too.'

'Meyowwwl,' came Benjamin's sad little voice. *Help!*

'We've got to do something,' I said. Then I thought of Laine. Maybe Laine was tall enough to reach the lower branches.

'I'll go and get Laine,' I said.

'She won't help,' Amanda said.

'Oh, yes she will,' I told Amanda. 'Just you wait here.'

I ran up the backyard and across into our house. Laine was sitting in the living room watching TV.

'Did you find him?' she asked.

'Yes.'

'There! Didn't I tell you!' Laine said. 'All that fuss!'

'He's up a tree and he can't get down,' I said. 'Amanda and I aren't tall enough to go up there after him.' I gave her a meaningful look. '*You* are.'

'Oh, come on, Stacy,' Laine said. 'Look, I'm sorry if you got upset about him being missing, and I'll even promise not to cover the cat-flap again. But if you think I'm climbing up a tree to bring him down, you must be out of your mind.'

'Are you sure you don't want to help?' I said.

'He'll come down when he's ready,' Laine said. 'Cats are like that. Besides, I'm waiting for a phone call. I can't help you, Stacy. Matt's going to call me at any minute.'

I looked at her. 'Have you been sitting by the phone all day?' I asked.

She shifted awkwardly in her seat. 'I know he'll call,' she said.

'Why don't you call him?' I asked.

She shook her head. 'No! He's got to call me.'

'It'll only take a minute to get Benjamin down,' I said. 'Please, Laine?'

She looked at the telephone. 'OK,' she said, getting up. 'OK, I'll help. I don't care if he *does* call. I don't want to talk to him anyway.'

She spends the day sitting by the phone waiting for her boyfriend to call – and then she says she doesn't want to talk to him anyway? And this is the person that Amanda wants to grow up to be like!

Chapter Fifteen

Things were a little chilly between Amanda and Laine as the three of us stood at the foot of the Lloyds' tree and looked up into the branches.

'Have you tried tempting him down with some food?' Laine asked.

'Oh, gee, we never thought of that!' Amanda said sarcastically. 'Aren't *we* the dumb ones!'

Laine gave her an icy look.

'Can't you climb up there?' I asked Laine.

'I can *try*,' Laine said. She jumped up and caught hold of one of the lowest branches. Her fingers slipped off.

'You'll have to help me,' she gasped. 'I'm not very good at things like this. Give me a push.'

She jumped again and managed to grab hold of the branch. Amanda and I took a leg each and gave her a good shove. Up she went into the leaves, pulling herself up over the branch and scrabbling to get a foothold.

The branches swayed and rustled as Laine got herself up into the tree.

'Can you see him?' I called up to her.

'Nope,' Laine called down. 'Are you sure he's up here?'

'Of course we're sure,' Amanda said. 'We're not totally stupid.'

I heard Laine whimpering a little as she clambered up on to a high branch. Leaves and bits of twig rained down on us as we watched the bottom half of Laine squeezing up through the tangle of branches.

'Hah!' Laine gasped. 'Got you!'

'Have you found him?' I called.

'Yes,' Laine shouted down. 'He's right up near the top. I'm just going to . . . owww! Owwwch! Don't scratch, you stupid animal – I'm trying to rescue you!'

The tree swayed alarmingly.

'There he goes!' Amanda yelled.

Wow! I'd never seen anything like it. A grey shape suddenly appeared over on the far side of the tree. The branch dipped.

'Benjamin!' I hollered. 'Careful!' He took a flying leap toward the fence. 'Eek!' I yelled. He made a perfect landing on the fence and bounced down into our backyard. I ran over to the fence and saw him go speeding toward the house and in through the back door.

'Yesss!' I yelled. 'Laine, you did it!'

There was a lot of heaving about going on up in the tree.

'Guys,' Laine called down. 'I could do with a little *help*.'

'It's OK,' Amanda called. 'He jumped down.' There was more rustling and swaying from the top of the tree.

'You can come down now,' I called.

'I *can't*!' Laine howled.

'Why not?' Amanda called.

'I'm stuck!'

Amanda and I looked at each other and grinned.

'Guys?' Laine wailed. 'I'm really stuck. *Do* something.'

Amanda looked at me. 'What do you say, Stacy?' she asked teasingly. 'Should we leave her up there?'

'I guess we could throw food up to her every now and then,' I said.

'I don't know what two *kids* can do to help,' Amanda called up to Laine. 'I mean, it takes a real grown-up person to deal with something like this.'

'Come on, guys,' Laine called down. 'Stop fooling around!'

'But I'm a kid,' Amanda called. 'What can *I* do?'

'You're not a kid,' Laine shouted. 'Think of something!'

'I'm not?' Amanda called. 'Are you *sure* about that?'

'Yes,' Laine called. 'You're not a kid at all. Come on, you guys – this is very uncomfortable!'

Amanda looked at me. 'I guess we could get the ladder out of the garage,' she said.

'Get the ladder!' Laine howled, and then she gave this real loud sneeze. 'Please,' she moaned. 'Go get the ladder.'

'Are you going to be nice to Benjamin from now on?' I called.

'Yes. I promise.'

'And I'm *not* a kid?' Amanda called.

'No, you're not a kid,' Laine called down before she let out another sneeze.

Amanda smiled at me. 'I guess we'd better fetch the ladder,' she said.

It took us a few minutes to get it out of our garage and carry it into the Lloyds' backyard. We propped it up against the tree and Amanda climbed up. Laine had gotten really tangled up in the branches, but with Amanda's help she finally got herself free.

'*Atishoo!*' Laine's eyes were red and streaming as she flopped down on the ground under the tree. 'Urgh! I got a faceful of – *atishoo!* – cat hair! ATISHOO!'

'It does *that* to you?' I said, seeing how her face had gone all red and her eyes had puffed up.

'I told you!' Laine moaned. 'I'm *allergic*!'

'I thought you just meant you didn't like cats,' I said.

Laine wiped her eyes. 'Would *you* like cats if they did *this* to you? Urrgh!' She clambered to her feet. 'Is he OK?'

'I think so,' I said. 'Hey, I'm sorry, Laine. I didn't realize you were really allergic.'

'Oh, that's OK,' Laine groaned, rubbing her sleeve across her eyes. 'Look, guys – can we be friends again? Can we just forget about everything that's happened and be *friends* again?'

Amanda and I looked at each other.

'I guess so,' Amanda said. 'But will you take me to a disco just as soon as I'm old enough?'

'It's a deal,' Laine said. 'On your sixteenth birthday I'll take you to as many discos as you like! *Atishoo!*'

'And I'll make sure Benjamin keeps away from you,' I said. 'It's going to take a bit of *explaining* to him – but I'll do my best.'

Laine smiled and put her arms around us.

'Can we still go to the movies?' I asked. 'You said you'd take us. And I know what movie I want to see.'

'Of course,' Laine said. 'But I'll need a few minutes to take a shower and get all this cat hair off me.'

The three of us took the ladder back to our garage.

'What movie are we going to see?' Amanda asked.

'*Out of the Wild*,' I said.

'But that's a kids' film!' Amanda said.

'So let's all go and see a kids' film,' Laine said to Amanda. 'Even grown-ups like us can enjoy a good kids' film sometimes.'

Amanda laughed. 'I guess so,' she said. 'Come on, guys. Last one ready pays for the popcorn!'

* * *

'Well, I'm glad you all had a good time,' Mom said. She smiled at Laine. 'I've got to admit, I wondered how you'd cope with this pair of crazies.'

'They were both terrific,' Laine said. 'No problem at all. I really enjoyed myself.'

It was Friday afternoon. Mom had been back about an hour. Grandma was doing fine and Aunt Susie had taken over for the weekend. Mom told us that by next week Gran would be able to get around well enough not to need looking after any more.

Amanda and I were on the living-room rug, playing with Sam. I hadn't realized how much I'd missed him until I saw him in Mom's arms. We had a whole week of catching up to do.

We'd had a great time at the movies the night before, and on the way home Laine had taken us out for a pizza. We didn't get home until after eleven o'clock!

Mom was about to take Laine off to the train station when I remembered the vase.

Amanda and I handed it over together.

'It's beautiful,' Mom said, taking it out of the wrapping paper. She put it on the table by the window. 'Doesn't that look fine!' she said. 'Who picked it out?'

'We all did,' I said.

We all went to the train station to say goodbye to Laine. It was nice that things were going to be back to normal at home, but I was going to miss Laine, despite all the stuff that had happened. After all – everything had worked out fine in the end.

'Come and visit soon,' Amanda said.

'Try and stop me,' Laine smiled. She gave Amanda a big hug and Amanda went back to the car.

'Maybe you could take something for your cat allergy?' I said. 'Pills or something?'

'I'll try that,' Laine said, hugging me. 'And I'll come over to see you real soon, OK?'

'OK!' I said. And I meant it.

* * *

It was Sunday afternoon and I was in my room rearranging my frog collection to include a new one that Dad had brought back from New York.

'Hey, Stacy?' Amanda stuck her head around the door. 'Do you still have those pictures of Eddie Eden that I gave you?'

'I thought you wanted me to throw them out,' I said. 'I thought you didn't like Eddie Eden any more.'

Amanda came into my room. 'That was only for a little while,' she said. 'But I like him again now. So I'd like my CD back as well.' She looked at me. 'What do you think of Laine?'

'She's OK,' I said.

'I guess so,' Amanda said. 'But, you know, I always used to think she was so perfect. I wanted to be just like her.'

I grinned. 'Really?' I said. 'I'd never have guessed!'

Amanda gave me a dismissive wave of her hand. 'There are things about her I still like. Her hair, for instance – and the fact that she's old enough to learn to drive. But she's such a feeb! The way she got stuck up that tree!'

'I guess she *is* kind of girly,' I said. 'And the way she was just sitting there waiting for Matt to call! Yuck! I mean she's five years older than you, and she's sitting around waiting for some guy to call her?'

Amanda nodded. 'And anyway,' she said, 'who wants to spend an hour a day slapping on make-up that will get all messed up after five minutes of cheerleading?'

I laughed. 'Can you imagine Laine doing anything as energetic as cheerleading?' I said.

'Not really,' Amanda said. 'Do I get my posters back now?'

'I guess so,' I said. I opened my closet and brought out the roll of pictures that Laine had given me.

'You can listen to the CD any time you like.

Just ask.' She took the bundle of pictures from me. 'It's just too bad Laine doesn't appreciate good music, that's all I can say!'

I grinned. 'Yeah,' I said. 'I guess it is.'

* * *

It was Saturday afternoon, about two weeks later.

Honk! Honk! A car horn out front.

'What the heck is that?' Dad asked, looking out of the window. 'Hey, girls – take a look at this!' he said.

We ran over to the window. There was a bright shiny new car parked out front. The driver's door opened and Laine got out.

'It's Laine!' Amanda and I shouted. We ran to the front door and out into the driveway.

'Hi!' Laine shouted. 'I passed my test! First time! And Mom bought me this car!'

We raced down to give her a hug.

'That's great, Laine!' Mom called from the doorway. 'This calls for a celebration! Come on in!'

'Hi, Aunt Barbara!' Laine called, waving. 'Hi, Uncle David! Can I take Amanda and Stacy out for a ride?' She looked at us. 'Would you like that?'

A ride in Laine's new car! We didn't need asking twice.

'I want to sit up front!' Amanda said, before I could get a word in.

'Not fair!' I said. 'We should draw straws to see who rides in the front!' Typical Amanda!

'Hey, no arguing, you two,' Laine said with a smile. 'Amanda can ride up front on the way, and Stacy gets to ride up front on the way back. OK?'

Mom and Dad waved as we climbed into the car.

'Where are we going?' I asked.

'Where would you like to go?' Laine said.

'Cruising around town!' Amanda said. (Yeah, right! In the hope that some of her friends might see her.)

'Out into the country!' I said.

Laine started the engine. 'We'll do *both*,' she said. 'And then we'll stop off somewhere and I'll buy you the biggest ice-cream sundae you've ever seen!'

We waved at Mom and Dad as Laine drove out of the driveway and we headed off down the road.

You know something? I wouldn't have believed it was possible – but it seems to me that people *can* be really nice, even if they *don't* get along so well with cats.

Just don't tell Benjamin I said so, OK?

Stacy and Amanda are back in **Little Sister Book 5**, *Sneaking Out*, coming soon from Red Fox. Here's a sneak preview:

Chapter One

You know what it's like. You open a magazine and this big movie star or rock star smiles out at you from the pool side or from a beach in the Bahamas. Somewhere really sunny and hot and fabulous.

The writing under the photo always says something like: *Babs Morello takes time off from shooting her next blockbuster movie to relax at her Bermuda beach house.* Or, *Paulie Peters hangs out with fans before his next sell-out concert in San Francisco.*

And you look out of the window in Four Corners, Indiana, and the sky is grey, and you've got some incredibly difficult homework to finish and hand in tomorrow or else Ms Fenwick will go crazy. And baby Sam is crying; and no matter *how* much you love him, it's still driving you nuts!

And these glamorous people smile up at you out of the magazine with their suntans and their perfect teeth. And you just have to *do something* to even things up a little.

So you take out a pen and draw a pair of glasses on the picture. You just can't help yourself. Who cares if it's a really childish thing to do? Who cares if you're ten years old and you're acting like you're *six*. And then you blank out a couple of front teeth and give Babs or Pauline a really dumb haircut. A bolt through the neck, like Frankenstein's monster, a couple of good scars and some stubble.

It is *so* satisfying to do that!

And that was all I was doing when my sister Amanda came in and started screaming the house down.

'Stacy!' she yelled. 'I wanted that picture!'

I nearly jumped out of my chair. I'd been concentrating so hard on customizing Eddie Eden's photo that I hadn't even noticed she was breathing down my neck until she nearly deafened me by yelling right in my ear.

I've got to admit. I felt pretty embarrassed. I mean, drawing silly faces on photographs isn't exactly the most grown-up thing to be caught doing.

'Don't sneak up on me like that!' I said. 'You've already got twenty-three million pictures of Eddie Eden.'

'I don't have *that* picture!' Amanda said. 'I asked Mom to save that magazine for me. I asked her *especially*!'

'No one told me anything about it,' I said. 'Anyway – it's an improvement. In fact, if you want me to, I can go up to your room right now and make some improvements to all the others.'

'You're a rat, Stacy Allen.' Amanda said. 'Just you wait until you find something in life that's important to you! Just you wait!'

She turned and walked out of the kitchen. I heard her run upstairs and slam her bedroom door.

As fights between Amanda and me go, that was pretty tame. Usually, Amanda is a whole lot more feisty than that.

I knew *why* she wasn't feeling up to having a proper yelling-match with me. It had to do with Eddie Eden.

You see, Eddie Eden was on tour right then. He was taking his show right across America. It was called the 'This Way to Paradise' tour, and he was playing a couple of nights really close to where we live. One concert was actually going to be in Four Corners, and the other in Mayville, which is only a few miles away.

I guess you're wondering why that should be a problem.

The problem was that the theater in Four Corners is way over on the far side of town and Mom and Dad said Amanda couldn't go. They said she was too young to go to a rock concert.

(Mom said, 'Maybe, next year, honey.' Next *year*? I don't believe the way parents sometimes come out with stuff like that. Next *year* – like it's only just around the corner. What kind of a person can wait an entire year for something? Even I could sympathize with Amanda on that one.)

Amanda had been kind of down about it for the last few weeks. She'd tried to talk them into letting her go. She'd tried bargaining with them – you know. 'If I get a B+ for my science project, can I go to the concert?' She'd even tried convincing them that she'd be *ill* if she couldn't go. But nothing worked. She wasn't going to the concert, and that was that.

I hadn't doodled over that picture of Eddie Eden to upset her all over again. I didn't know she wanted it. She really has got pictures of him all over her room. You'd think one more or less wouldn't matter.

I tried de-customizing the picture with an

eraser, but all I managed to do was to rub a hole clean through the page – taking Eddie's top front tooth with it.

Now I'm not always in line for a '*Sister of the Year*' award, but I was feeling kind of sorry for Amanda – as well as feeling a little guilty that I hadn't apologized for messing up her picture. And this was one time when I could actually do something to put things right – at least as far as the photograph was concerned.

I called down to the basement, where Mom has her office. 'Mom. I'm just going out for ten minutes.'

'OK, honey,' Mom called back.

Mom works as a manuscript proofreader. She's got a proper little office down in our basement, with a word processor and every-thing. Proofreading is the kind of job that can be done from home, which means she can be around for Sam and us and earn money at the same time. Which is kind of useful when there's not a whole lot of spare cash around, what with diapers and toys for Sam, oil-paints and brushes for Amanda and my monthly mail-order wildlife books.

I went down to the store and bought another copy of the magazine with that picture of Eddie Eden in it.

I bought a candy bar, too. After all, if I'm doing a good deed for Amanda, I ought to get *some* kind of reward.

Back home, I went upstairs and knocked on Amanda's bedroom door.

'Amanda? It's me-ee! Your favourite sister. I've got something for you,' I called.

'Go away,' Amanda said through the closed door. 'I'm not talking to you.'

'You *will* be when you see what I've got,' I said.

I folded the magazine open to the page with the photo of Eddie Eden.

Amanda snatched the door open. 'Why don't you just . . . oh!' She stood blinking at the photo. 'Oh . . . you cleaned it all off.'

I grinned at her. 'Who's a rat, Amanda? Am I still a rat, huh?'

She smiled. 'No, you're not a rat,' she said.

'Are you going to cut it out and pin it up, then?' I asked. 'Or are you planning on keeping it under your pillow with those buttons and postcards?'

'I do not keep buttons and postcards under my pillow,' Amanda said. She grinned. 'Well – only the *one* postcard.'

I went into her room. Gee! Talk about a *shrine* to Eddie Eden. There were posters and double-page spreads from magazines. There were black-and-white newspaper pictures and coloured pictures cut out of TV guides. And on one wall she had pinned up a whole bunch of her own drawings of him – taken from pictures. I was surprised she even had room for another picture – unless she was planning on glueing it to the ceiling!

I sat on her bed while she cut out the picture.

I've got to admit. I was feeling pretty good about myself. *Come on down, Stacy Allen – selfless sister of the semester!* Of course, this good deed also meant Amanda *owed* me one, which is always a good position to be in. Amanda could do me a favour sometime.

But it wasn't long before I found out that it wasn't Amanda who was going to be doing me a big favour in the near future. It was going to be entirely the other way round!

Other great reads ❦ *from* **Red Fox**

Further Red Fox titles that you might enjoy reading are listed on the following pages. They are available in bookshops or they can be ordered directly from us.

If you would like to order books, please send this form and the money due to:

ARROW BOOKS, BOOKSERVICE BY POST, PO BOX 29, DOUGLAS, ISLE OF MAN, BRITISH ISLES. Please enclose a cheque or postal order made out to Arrow Books Ltd for the amount due, plus 75p per book for postage and packing to a maximum of £7.50, both for orders within the UK. For customers outside the UK, please allow £1.00 per book.

NAME_____

ADDRESS_____

_____

Please print clearly.

Whilst every effort is made to keep prices low, it is sometimes necessary to increase cover prices at short notice. If you are ordering books by post, to save delay it is advisable to phone to confirm the correct price. The number to ring is THE SALES DEPARTMENT 071 (if outside London) 973 9700.

Other great reads *from Red Fox*

Little Sister Series by Alan Frewin Jones

LITTLE SISTER 1 – THE GREAT SISTER WAR

Meet Stacy Allen, a ten year old tomboy and a bit of a bookworm. *Now* meet her blue-eyed blonde sister, Amanda, just turned 13 and a fully-fledged teenager. Stacy thinks Amanda's a total airhead and Amanda calls Stacy and her gang the nerds; they have the biggest love-hate relationship of the century and that can only mean one thing – war.
ISBN 0 09 938381 0   £2.99

LITTLE SISTER 2 – MY SISTER, MY SLAVE

When Amanda starts to become a school slacker, Mom is ready to take drastic action – pull Amanda out of the cheerleading squad! So the sisters make a deal; Stacy will help Amanda with her school work in return for two whole days of slavery. But Amanda doesn't realize that when her little sister's boss, two days means 48 *whole* hours of chores – snea-kee!
ISBN 0 09 938391 8   £2.99

LITTLE SISTER 3 – STACY THE MATCHMAKER

Amanda is mad that the school Barbie doll, Judy McWilliams, has got herself a boyfriend, and to make things worse it's hunky Greg Masterson, the guy Amanda has fancied for ages. Stacy feels that it's her duty as sister to fix Amanda's lovelife and decides to play cupid and do a bit of matchmaking, with disastrous results!
ISBN 0 09 938401 9   £2.99

LITTLE SISTER 4 – COPYCAT

Cousin Laine is so coo-ol! She's a glamorous 18 year old and wears gorgeous clothes, and has got a boyfriend with a car. When Stacy and Amanda's parents go away for a week leaving Laine in charge, 13 year old Amanda decides she wants to be just like her cousin and begins to copy Laine's every move . . .
ISBN 0 09 938411 6   £2.99

BESTSELLING FICTION FROM RED FOX

☐	The Present Takers	Aidan Chambers	£2.99
☐	Battle for the Park	Colin Dann	£2.99
☐	Orson Cart Comes Apart	Steve Donald	£1.99
☐	The Last Vampire	Willis Hall	£2.99
☐	Harvey Angell	Diana Hendry	£2.99
☐	Emil and the Detectives	Erich Kästner	£2.99
☐	Krindlekrax	Philip Ridley	£2.99

PRICES AND OTHER DETAILS ARE LIABLE TO CHANGE

ARROW BOOKS, BOOKSERVICE BY POST, PO BOX 29, DOUGLAS, ISLE OF MAN, BRITISH ISLES

NAME ....

ADDRESS ....

....

....

Please enclose a cheque or postal order made out to B.S.B.P. Ltd. for the amount due and allow the following for postage and packing:

U.K. CUSTOMERS: Please allow 75p per book to a maximum of £7.50

B.F.P.O. & EIRE: Please allow 75p per book to a maximum of £7.50

OVERSEAS CUSTOMERS: Please allow £1.00 per book.

While every effort is made to keep prices low it is sometimes necessary to increase cover prices at short notice. Arrow Books reserve the right to show new retail prices on covers which may differ from those previously advertised in the text or elsewhere.

BESTSELLING FICTION FROM RED FOX

- [ ] The Story of Doctor Dolittle   Hugh Lofting   £3.99
- [ ] Amazon Adventure   Willard Price   £3.99
- [ ] Swallows and Amazons   Arthur Ransome   £3.99
- [ ] The Wolves of Willoughby Chase   Joan Aiken   £2.99
- [ ] Steps up the Chimney   William Corlett   £2.99
- [ ] The Snow-Walker's Son   Catherine Fisher   £2.99
- [ ] Redwall   Brian Jacques   £3.99
- [ ] Guilty!   Ruth Thomas   £2.99

PRICES AND OTHER DETAILS ARE LIABLE TO CHANGE

ARROW BOOKS, BOOKSERVICE BY POST, PO BOX 29,
DOUGLAS, ISLE OF MAN, BRITISH ISLES

NAME ....

ADDRESS ....

....

....

Please enclose a cheque or postal order made out to B.S.B.P. Ltd. for the amount due and allow the following for postage and packing:

U.K. CUSTOMERS: Please allow 75p per book to a maximum of £7.50

B.F.P.O. & EIRE: Please allow 75p per book to a maximum of £7.50

OVERSEAS CUSTOMERS: Please allow £1.00 per book.

While every effort is made to keep prices low it is sometimes necessary to increase cover prices at short notice. Arrow Books reserve the right to show new retail prices on covers which may differ from those previously advertised in the text or elsewhere.

BESTSELLING FICTION FROM RED FOX

☐	Blood	Alan Durant	£3.50
☐	Tina Come Home	Paul Geraghty	£3.50
☐	Del-Del	Victor Kelleher	£3.50
☐	Paul Loves Amy Loves Christo	Josephine Poole	£3.50
☐	If It Weren't for Sebastian	Jean Ure	£3.50
☐	You'll Never Guess the End	Barbara Wersba	£3.50
☐	The Pigman	Paul Zindel	£3.50

PRICES AND OTHER DETAILS ARE LIABLE TO CHANGE

ARROW BOOKS, BOOKSERVICE BY POST, PO BOX 29, DOUGLAS, ISLE OF MAN, BRITISH ISLES

NAME...

ADDRESS...

....

....

Please enclose a cheque or postal order made out to B.S.B.P. Ltd. for the amount due and allow the following for postage and packing:

U.K. CUSTOMERS: Please allow 75p per book to a maximum of £7.50

B.F.P.O. & EIRE: Please allow 75p per book to a maximum of £7.50

OVERSEAS CUSTOMERS: Please allow £1.00 per book.

While every effort is made to keep prices low it is sometimes necessary to increase cover prices at short notice. Arrow Books reserve the right to show new retail prices on covers which may differ from those previously advertised in the text or elsewhere.

Other great reads ~ *from* **Red Fox**

Teenage thrillers from Red Fox

GOING TO EGYPT   Helen Dunmore

When Dad announces they're going on holiday to
Weston, Colette is disappointed – she'd much rather
be going to Egypt. But when she meets the boys who
ride their horses in the sea at dawn, she realizes that
it isn't where you go that counts, it's who you meet
while you're there . . .
ISBN 0 09 910901 8   £3.50

BLOOD   Alan Durant

Life turns frighteningly upside down when Robert hears
his parents have been shot dead in the family home. The
police, the psychiatrists, the questions . . . Robert
decides to carry out his own investigations, and pushes
his sanity to the brink.
ISBN 0 09 992330 0   £3.50

DEL-DEL   Victor Kelleher

Des, Hannah and their children are a close-knit family
– or so it seems. But suddenly, a year after the death
of their daughter Laura, Sam the youngest son starts
to act very strangely – having been possessed by a
terrifyingly evil presence called Del-Del.
ISBN 0 09 918271 8   £3.50

THE GRANITE BEAST   Ann Coburn

After her father's death, Ruth is uprooted from town-
life to a close-knit Cornish village and feels lost and
alone. But the strange and terrifying dreams she has
every night are surely from something more than just
unhappiness? Only Ben, another outsider, seems to
understand the omen of major disaster . . .
ISBN 0 09 985970 X   £2.99